I0664830

AN ISOLATED *Range*

ANDREW GREY

Dreamspinner Press

Published by
Dreamspinner Press
382 NE 191st Street #88329
Miami, FL 33179-3899, USA
http://www.dreamspinnerpress.com/

Cover Art by L.C. Chase http://www.lcchase.com

ISBN: 978-1-62380-076-5

Printed in the United States of America
First Edition
December 2012

eBook edition available
eBook ISBN: 978-1-62380-077-2

Readers love Andrew Grey

A Foreign Range

"Mr. Grey is the master at building sexual tension between his characters, but there is always the emotional attachment as well that just makes the romantic in me give a deep and satisfied sigh at the end of his books."

—Guilty Indulgence

"Run—don't walk—to Dreamspinner or any online book vendor and grab your copy of *A Foreign Range* and get ready to ride the trails with these sexy cowboys."

—Dawn's Reading Nook

A Troubled Range

"This is one book that I won't forget and you shouldn't miss it."

—Fallen Angel Reviews

"…a solid, sweetly romantic and delightful story that will leave you clamoring for more after the last page is read."

—Love Romances and More

A Shared Range

"This is one of those stories to read when your heart is bruised and your world feels dark. You'll take a deep breath afterwards and see the sun again."

—Long and Short Reviews (Whipped Cream Reviews)

"…another enjoyable read filled with two well rounded and likable guys in Dakota and Wally, a great premise, a beautifully described mountain locale and two fun and interesting supporting characters."

—Literary Nymphs

Novels by ANDREW GREY

Accompanied by a Waltz
Dutch Treat
The Good Fight
Three Fates (anthology)
Work Me Out (anthology)

ART SERIES
Legal Artistry • Artistic Appeal • Artistic Pursuits • Legal Tender

BOTTLED UP STORIES
Bottled Up • Uncorked • The Best Revenge • An Unexpected Vintage

CHILDREN OF BACCHUS STORIES
Children of Bacchus • Thursday's Child • Child of Joy

LOVE MEANS... SERIES
Love Means... No Shame • Love Means... Courage • Love Means... No Boundaries
Love Means... Freedom • Love Means ... No Fear
Love Means... Family • Love Means... Renewal

SEVEN DAYS STORIES
Seven Days • Unconditional Love

STORIES FROM THE RANGE
A Shared Range • A Troubled Range • An Unsettled Range
A Foreign Range • An Isolated Range

TASTE OF LOVE STORIES
A Taste of Love • A Serving of Love • A Helping of Love • A Slice of Love

Novellas by ANDREW GREY

A Present in Swaddling Clothes • Snowbound in Nowhere

BY FIRE SERIES
Redemption by Fire • Strengthened by Fire • Burnished by Fire

CHILDREN OF BACCHUS STORIES
Spring Reassurance • Winter Love

LOVE MEANS... SERIES
Love Means... Healing • Love Means... Renewal

WORK OUT SERIES
Spot Me • Pump Me Up • Core Training • Crunch Time
Positive Resistance • Personal Training

All published by
DREAMSPINNER PRESS

To the basketball player from Gettysburg College who served as the inspiration for Marty. Your courage and dedication demonstrates what athletics are truly all about.

Chapter One

MARTY GREEN sat with the other players on Wyoming's Brackett College basketball team. The team bench was packed as they all waited for the game to begin. Marty imagined that all the other freshmen sitting near him felt the same butterflies in their stomachs that he did. Marty loved basketball—it was one of the honest and true passions in his life. That, and science. He was thrilled to have made the basketball team, even if he was destined to spend much of the season sitting on the bench. Marty knew he didn't have the talent to make it to the pros or even to get into one of the Division I basketball programs, but he didn't really care. He played because he loved the game and loved being on a team. He played because it was in his blood, and because there were those times when he and the ball seemed connected, when everything went exactly right. He lived for those times.

The starters were called to the court, and Marty watched as they ran out and got into position. Marty felt the excitement inside him ramp up. These were his teammates, and even though he wasn't playing, energy coursed through him. His legs bounced slightly, and he could feel the blood rushing from head to toe. It was like the energy from the entire crowd had centered on him, and he loved it.

The ball was tipped, and play began with his teammates in control of the ball. They raced down the court, dribbling and passing the ball rapidly back and forth in a dance that Marty desperately wanted to be a part of, but he could only wait and hope. A shot was taken, and they scored. The other guys on the bench all turned to one another, smiling, sharing their teammates' success as they watched, waited, and hoped that they'd eventually get their turn.

They were ahead at halftime. Granted, they were playing Cheyenne, a school slightly smaller than theirs, and one they fully expected to beat. The starters had been rotated out of the game early on, and the second string had still been able to score. The team filed back into the locker room to wait out the halftime while the crowd was entertained by the cheerleaders. After a pep talk, the team returned to the floor and waited for the game to resume. The coach pointed down the bench, and Marty hoped he'd be chosen, but of course he wasn't. Play began for the second half with many of their best players resting. One of the starters, Kyle, sat next to Marty, with his friend Pat on the other side. Kyle was a senior and he watched the play with eagle eyes.

"He'll never make the shot," Kyle said, motioning toward the player from the other team as he was about to lift off. "His feet aren't in the right position and he's a little off balance." Sure enough, the ball skimmed around the edge of the rim and then fell back into play, with Mike scooping it up and racing full-tilt down the court with the rest of the players behind him. Mike made the shot easily, and Brackett pulled further ahead. Play continued, and Kyle continued his quiet narrative, pointing things out to Marty that he might have missed. "You learn by doing and by seeing other guys' mistakes," Kyle said just before throwing the towel he'd had hanging around his neck onto the bench and hurrying back into the game.

Marty watched as the second half continued. They were way ahead now, and as more players came out, Marty heard what he'd hoped for: "Green, you're in," the coach said, and Marty hurried onto the court just as the other team called time. The other team's players all huddled around their coach, and for a few seconds, Marty thought he could hear what their coach was saying.

Everything seemed heightened—the sound of the crowd, the voices of the other players—and as he looked over at his coach, he swore he could hear him telling him to stay in the pocket from all the way across the court. Marty knew he had to be hearing things, that he was so keyed up and hypersensitive about playing in his first college game that it had to be his imagination.

The refs signaled the resumption of play, and Marty got his head in the game, paying close attention to the ball and everyone around him. The whistle blew and the ball was in play. Marty knew his assignment and guarded his player while looking for an opening. The ball was passed his way, but one of the other players on his team scooped it off its trajectory and rocketed down the court. Marty followed, his feet pounding on the polished floor, ready to assist if he could, but the shot was good and they scored. Then the other team had the ball, and Marty stayed close to his man when the ball came their way. Marty wasn't able to get it, but he did manage to bounce it off the other player and out of bounds, forcing a turnover to their team. The ref handed him the ball, and he stepped out of bounds. This was the first time in an actual college game that he'd had possession of the ball. Marty passed it to Clark and jumped into the play, following the others down the court. Clark passed the ball, and then it was passed back to him. Marty watched as a shot was taken, but it missed and then one of his teammates rebounded the ball and put it back in the basket for a score. They were doing well, but he knew his time was limited. There were others guys who needed their chance to play, and if he wanted to stay in, Marty needed to make something happen.

The other team had possession, and he stepped away from his man, watching the ball as it was passed over. Realizing he'd created the opening, Marty instantly closed it and snatched the ball out of the air. He dribbled it and then began running down the court. He felt almost at one with the ball, blood pumping, legs pounding, arms working as he reached the far side of the court and got into position.

Suddenly, almost like a fuse had blown, Marty's head throbbed and his balance seemed all out of whack. He tried to steady himself with his left arm, but it didn't seem to want to work. He stopped moving and looked around for a player to pass the ball to, but everything in the room looked distorted. The ball was snatched out of his hand, and Marty could vaguely hear his name being called, but it was like listening through Jell-O and he couldn't make out anything else. He knew which way the bench was and he took one step. He lifted his left leg and set it down, but he seemed to keep going. He realized he was falling and he could do nothing at all to stop it. He tried, but his muscles ignored the commands his brain sent out, and then he collapsed onto the court.

Marty heard activity all around him. He tried to get up but couldn't. All he could see was the ceiling above him, the celebratory banners waving and then starting to move in weird patterns. He could hear voices around him, but they weren't making any sense, their words jumbled and all mixed up. Marty couldn't take the weird sights going on above him, so he closed his eyes, hoping it would help, but it didn't. The entire world seemed to have gone haywire. He knew people were talking to him, asking him questions that he tried to answer, but even his thoughts seemed mixed up and confused. Finally, he gave up and gave himself over to the people around him. Whatever was going on, he would have to trust that they knew what was happening, because he didn't.

The only thing that seemed to permeate the haze that surrounded him was the sensation of flying. He liked that—it felt good. Marty tried to put out his arms so he could fly faster, but he couldn't seem to, so he gave up and let himself fly wherever he was going. Slowly, the world got darker, and Marty didn't fight it. He needed to sleep, and he hoped that after he woke up the world would be right again.

"Stay with us, Marty," someone said, and Marty opened his eyes for a few seconds, but everything was strange and still swimmy, so he closed them again and kept them that way. People said more things to him, but he wasn't really interested. He didn't understand most of what they were saying, anyway. All he wanted to do was sleep, and as he gave in to it, the world turned black as Marty embraced the silence.

MARTY'S dreams were jumbles of half-grasped images and sounds that made absolutely no sense. Sometimes he dreamed he was playing basketball at the school near his house with all of his friends. Some of them were older, like him, and some were seven and eight years old. He tried to make sense of the dreams, but he couldn't. He tried to make the dreams stop, or at least make sense, but they refused.

"Marty, wake up for me," he heard from outside, and he tried to move toward the sound because it was the only thing that made any sense to him, but he couldn't. Every time he got close, there was something there, and when he tried to break through, it got stronger and stronger. The voice would sometimes call again, and Marty would get closer, but it wasn't quite enough.

"Marty, it's me. Wake up for me, honey." He knew that voice—it was his mother. It was the first thing he'd ever recognized from his swirling dreams. He had to get to her. He tried again, and this time the mists parted, but he couldn't quite reach it. "Open your eyes," he heard, and Marty did.

The room was dim, and all he could see was a tiled ceiling, but then someone leaned over him and he saw what might have been a head, but he wasn't sure. He heard voices talking, but they were all a bit jumbled and overlapping. He finally could make out words and phrases, though.

"Oh, honey," he heard his mother say, and Marty tried to smile, at least he thought he was smiling. Part of his body felt detached and weird. "Call the doctor," his mother said, and Marty closed his eyes again. He could still hear the voices and he was determined not to go away again, but his eyelids felt so heavy.

"You're awake," a strange, deep voice said, and Marty opened his eyes as a man leaned over the bed. "That's very good. Can you follow the light?" Marty did his best and was able to follow the bright light with his eyes as it moved in front of him. "You're doing very well. I'm Dr. Feelgood." Marty liked that name. It sounded nice. "Can you feel this?" Marty felt a light touch on his right arm. "Move your hand if you can." Marty concentrated and felt his right hand move. He did it again, just to prove to himself that he could. "Very good. Can you feel this?" Marty felt cold on his leg and then a hand lightly touched his calf. "Move your leg if you can." Marty concentrated again and he felt his leg move slightly on the bedding. "Excellent."

Marty tried to speak, but he couldn't seem to. He tried something as simple as "yes," but what came out was slurred and he didn't understand himself.

"Can you feel my hand?" Marty felt a touch, and while he knew he felt something, it was hard for him to determine where the sensation was coming from. "Can you move your leg?" Marty tried moving his other leg, and for the life of him, he thought he was doing it, but he couldn't feel anything happening. "How about here?"

"Sssss," Marty said for yes.

"Go ahead and try to move your hand." Marty tried, and he swore in his mind he was waving his arm all around, but he didn't feel anything moving. That side of his body seemed sort of detached and lost, like it was there, but not there.

"Can you swallow for me?" For the first time, he saw the face of the man that went with the voice as he came into Marty's field of vision. Marty concentrated again, and he made his throat work. His throat scraped, and he wondered why he was swallowing sand, but he did it. "That's excellent. We'll start you on some ice chips and move you to liquids when you're ready."

"Sssss," Marty said, and the doctor smiled.

"Relax and take it easy. Your mother and father are here. I'll be back to see you later this evening." Marty felt the doctor lightly pat his arm and then move away. He heard soft voices, but was too tired to really care what anyone was saying.

"Honey, here's some ice," his mother said gently, entering his narrow field of vision. Something cold and soothing entered his mouth, and he closed his eyes as cold water dripped down his throat. Marty swallowed carefully, expecting the same pain he'd felt earlier. This time it wasn't as bad, and after a few seconds, he swallowed again. Each time felt better, and once the ice was gone, his mother placed another cube in his mouth.

"Ssss gggg www mmmm?" Marty asked. He'd meant to say "what's wrong with me."

"It's okay, honey, you're going to be fine. Just rest and sleep if you need to. I'll be right here, and I won't leave you." She sounded seconds from crying, and as she moved out of his line of sight, his dad leaned over the bed.

"You're doing great, sport. Take it easy, and we'll talk later, when things are better." Marty had never seen his father looking so worried or with such deep rings around his eyes. He knew what they were saying was a lie. Things weren't all right. He couldn't communicate, and the world still seemed to be in a bit of a fog, his thoughts jumbled and sort of like parts of his brain had been scrambled. Marty gave up and slowly closed his eyes, letting sleep overtake him once again.

The next time he woke, the room was nearly dark. He looked around and slowly turned his head. At least he could move that. He saw his mother asleep on a banquette beneath the dark windows. This time, his thoughts seemed somewhat clearer and less jumbled. He didn't try to talk, but he did try stringing sentences and thoughts together in his mind, which seemed much less like he was trying to think through cotton. "Mom," he tried to say, but it came out more like a groan.

"Honey?" she asked, stirring and then getting up. "Are you thirsty?" She lifted a cup with a straw to his lips. He tried to suck, but it seemed that whatever got into his mouth dribbled down his front. His mother wiped him up gently. "Try to close your mouth," she told him, and he had to concentrate, but he was finally able to drink without having water run down his chin. "That's good," she told him, and Marty felt like he was going to cry. What had happened to him to leave him so completely helpless?

She turned away and set the cup on a tray. He wanted to ask her so many things, but when he tried, he was only able to make grunts and moans that made him sound like an animal. Giving up, he closed his eyes again and silently wished for all this to be a nightmare and that the next time he woke up, everything would be back to normal.

"It's going to be okay, honey. Just give it time," his mother said, stroking his arm lightly as Marty tried not to cry and failed.

"YOU'RE doing a lot better," Dr. Feelgood—who he now knew was really Dr. Fielding—told him as he made his daily visit a few days later. Marty stared up at him. He could move his head, so at least now he could communicate yes and no answers. He'd also found out a number of different things. That he was being fed through a tube and that he was peeing into a bag and wore a diaper that had to be changed on a regular, and extremely embarrassing, basis.

"Wha happ-da?" Marty asked. Certain sounds were difficult for him to make, but he could at least form some basic words. He'd worked on it every chance he could get.

"You had a stroke," the doctor answered. "It's very rare in someone your age. It was probably something that could have happened at any time in your life."

"A soke?" Marty said, and the doctor nodded.

"Parts of your brain have been damaged, and that's why certain things are hard for you. But you're strong, and with time you should be able to recover a lot of what you lost. Your speech is already coming back, and in a few days, we'll bring in a speech therapist to help you. Once you're stronger, we'll also start you on physical therapy." Marty looked down at his left side. He'd already discovered that he could move his right hand and leg pretty well, but he could do very little with his left hand and leg. "The parts damaged mostly affect your left side. That's why you're having trouble talking. I think a lot of that will come back on its own, given the progress you've already made. But you need to give it time."

Marty wanted to ask about school, his friends, the team, but he knew all that would have to wait. "Ow log?" The doctor looked at his mother, and Marty repeated himself. "Ow log!"

"You've been in the hospital for ten days," his mother answered. "Christmas is in two days, and the whole family will be up here to celebrate it with you."

Ten days. He'd been like this for ten days, and all he could do was make grunting sounds and pee into a bag. Ten whole freaking days he'd been lying on his back able to do nothing, eating out of a tube. More than anything, Marty wanted to get the hell out of this bed. He wanted to see and talk to his friends. Ten whole days.

"It's okay, buddy. Your body and mind needed to process what had happened to it. You're going to get better from now on, so just relax and don't get upset." The doctor made some notes on the chart. "We're going to remove the feeding tube a little later today so you can have some food this evening." Marty nodded, feeling a bit mollified. He knew none of this was their fault; it was just a shock that he'd been out of it for so long. The doctor left the room, and Marty turned his head toward his mother.

"Visi-ors?" Marty asked. Over the last ten days he'd certainly had people visit, yet the room he was in was sparse, without flowers or cards.

"There have been people who asked, but we didn't want you disturbed," she said evenly, and Marty scowled at her. He knew what that meant. His parents hadn't allowed him any visitors because people might see him this way. Maybe they were right, but surely people had sent cards and stuff. There was nothing as far as he could see. "When you're stronger, you can have visitors."

If Marty had been strong enough, he would have argued with her, but he didn't have the energy. He should have known she and his father would act this way. Yes, he knew they had their reasons, but still. Marty sighed softly. When he was growing up, Marty's parents had regimented the lives of their children. Marty was the oldest and he'd been the first to go away to college. Those months had been glorious. He'd been able to do what he wanted and make friends with the people he wished, as opposed to the people his parents approved of. He should have known that as soon as he returned to his parents' home, they would close the door on any parts of his life that they didn't personally control. They'd always said it was for his own protection, which was why they lived on a massive plot of land behind fences and long private drives with guards and security guards who patrolled the perimeter of the property day and night. His father was a very important man, Marty knew that. He also knew his folks lived in fear of anything happening to their children, but what his parents had done in their zeal to protect them was cut them off from the outside world.

Marty's mother was a soft-spoken, small woman with a backbone of steel. She could politely tell someone to go to hell and they'd think it was a compliment, but no one ever crossed her. Closing his eyes again, he let sleep take him.

THE entire family did indeed show up for a very subdued and short Christmas celebration in his room. They opened gifts and talked while Marty lay in the bed. He could eat soft foods, and with his good arm, he managed to feed himself most of his dinner. He continually tried to use his other hand, and while he was able to move it somewhat, he found he had very little control. His leg was the same way, but he was determined to improve. Even though the doctor said he wasn't to overdo it, he found he was constantly trying to move his arm and leg. Thankfully, his speech had improved quickly, along with his control over his mouth, so his mother no longer needed to feed him.

Once the short party was over, Cassie and Josh, his little sister and brother, were taken home by his dad, but his mother remained in the room. "Go home," Marty told her.

"I'm not going to leave you," she said, but Marty could see the deep circles under her eyes. She was tired and she looked it.

"Go home," he reiterated. "Merry Christmas." The words were a bit slurred, and he wanted to tell her to go be with Cassie and Josh, that they needed her, but long thoughts were still difficult to get right. He turned on the television and began watching a movie. His comprehension and memory seemed to have come back really well. His biggest problem was his motor skills.

"Are you sure?"

"Yes," he told her, holding up the phone he'd begged her to get for him. Begging maybe wasn't the right description, since speech was still difficult, but he'd kept asking until she'd given in. "Go sleep," he told her, and she gathered her things and left the room after saying good-bye.

Harvey, one of the nurses, came in awhile later to check on him. "How are you doing?" he asked as he checked things over. "Is everything okay? You don't need anything changed?" Harvey was really nice about the whole diaper thing, which made Marty feel better. He hated it when his mother insisted on cleaning him up, and he'd finally convinced the hospital staff that it was to be on his chart that they do it. There were some things you would rather have strangers do than your mother.

"No, I'm good," he answered.

"Did your mother leave?" Harvey asked as he continued working, fluffing Marty's pillows and checking his back for sores.

"Yes," Marty answered. "Merry Christmas to me."

Harvey began to laugh. "She is a little clingy, isn't she?" Marty wanted to laugh as well, and he did as close an approximation as he could. "Since she's gone, is there anyone you want to wish a Merry Christmas to? I could help you make the call."

Marty got his best Christmas present that year from Harvey. He stayed for an hour and helped Marty call as many of his friends as he could, and when he got tired, Harvey made sure he was comfortable before leaving the room. "Thank you, Harvey," Marty said as his benefactor got ready to leave.

"You're welcome," Harvey told him, and Marty swallowed hard. "I know you're lonely and your mama's like a mother tiger." Harvey smiled and left the room. Marty turned his attention back to the television and watched it until he fell asleep.

Days turned to weeks. His nineteenth birthday came and went, and Marty spent much of that time in a hospital bed. He knew his parents were still not letting him have many visitors, which really chafed at him. He talked to his friends on the phone, but was hesitant to invite them to the hospital to visit because of the reception they seemed to be getting from his protective family. Until he'd gone away to college, he hadn't really realized just how insular his entire family had become. Growing up, he'd known his family was different, but he hadn't realized just how different until he'd been out of the house for a while.

"You're getting stronger, and your muscular movement and control are improving," Dr. Fielding told him during his regular morning visit. "I think you should start spending your days in your chair if you can."

Marty glared at the shiny new motorized wheelchair his family had gotten for him. It sat in the corner of the room, and he hated the thing. "Okay, but have them bring me a regular chair. I want to try to move myself." Marty was determined to use his left arm and leg again. His right side had improved to the point where he was almost back to normal, and thankfully, the left side of his face had slowly returned to where he could control it. He could speak clearly again and take care of himself to a certain degree. "How much longer do you think I'll be in here?" Marty asked as he shifted on the bed.

"Hopefully not much longer," Dr. Fielding said with a smile. "You should be able to get around on your own fairly well soon, and once you can do that, there's no reason for you to stay here any longer. I understand your parents are looking at having a room in their home converted to make things easier for you." The doctor made that sound like it was the greatest thing in the world, but all Marty could do was sigh. "You look like that's a bad thing," the doctor added as he finished with the chart and set it on the tray.

Marty eyed the doctor a bit suspiciously. "Before I say anything, I want to ask if you're my doctor or my parents' doctor."

"I'm your doctor," he answered, sitting in the chair next to Marty's bed.

"So anything I tell you is confidential?" Marty asked, and Dr. Fielding looked uncomfortable. "Thanks," Marty said, turning away. That expression told him all he needed to know.

"I'm your doctor, and I will not tell your parents anything you don't want them told," the doctor said with a bit of fire that Marty was glad to see. It took a strong person to be able to stand up to his dad, whether he was in the room or not.

"I don't want to go home to my parents' house. Not that it isn't nice and all, but I want to get better, and my parents will shelter and coddle me to the point where I'll go crazy. I'd almost rather go to a nursing home. You don't know any that have horses and a basketball court, do you?" Marty laughed slightly, but the doctor didn't break a smile. "Look, my family tends to be protective, too protective. I had to practically beg them to let me live in the dorm with the other guys."

"Yes," the doctor agreed. Almost everyone had heard the story of what had happened to Marty's baby brother. "Can you blame them?"

"Probably not," Marty agreed reluctantly. "But can you imagine what it's been like for the past five years? They live in constant fear of the same thing happening to another of their children, and I know my getting sick has played into my mother's fears. She stayed here with me for weeks, and it took a crowbar to get her to leave me alone for a while. For some reason, I think she blames the school and my friends for what happened to me. She knows it wasn't their fault, but she blames them and probably herself too. She told me once that she keeps thinking that if she had been there, maybe this wouldn't have happened." Marty paused, and the doctor nodded slowly.

"That's part of being a parent," the doctor said before adding, "For the record, there was nothing anyone could have done to prevent what happened to you. In fact, you were very lucky to have survived and to be doing as well as you are."

That wasn't news to Marty; he'd been told that before. "I know they love me and want the best for me, but I need to be away from them." Marty knew telling the doctor this probably wouldn't do much good. "I want to be independent. I have money of my own from a trust, so I can pay for my care if I need to."

"I'll make a deal with you," the doctor told him as he stood up. "If you get to the point where you can get yourself around in your chair, then I'll see what I can do." There was a curious look in the doctor's eye, and Marty wanted to ask what it was, but he heard his mother's footsteps coming down the hall and he knew if she got wind of his plans, she'd find a way to derail them fast. "Now, I'll send someone in to help you into your chair. I don't want you tiring yourself out," Dr. Fielding said with a wink before he left the room, greeting Marty's mother as he passed.

"How are you feeling?" his mother asked, setting her purse on the chair next to his bed. "Did I hear they're going to move you to your chair?" She looked at the chair in the corner and began moving it toward the bed.

"Not that one, Mom," Marty told her, and she stopped. "They're bringing a regular chair."

"But you're not ready for one of those yet," she said and proceeded to bring the motorized chair closer to the bed.

The orderly came in with the chair and his mother began to take over. “He’s going to use this one,” she said forcefully.

“No, I’m not. I’m using the regular chair.” Marty sat up and began scooting himself to the edge of the bed. He knew his mother was about to argue, but the orderly came over and gently lifted him out of the bed before carefully setting him in the chair. “Thank you,” he told the large man, and he smiled. “Could I get one of the pillows?” Marty asked after settling into the chair for a few seconds, and the orderly brought him one from the bed. Marty carefully leaned forward as the orderly placed it behind his back. “That’s better.”

It felt good to sit up again, and Marty leaned back in the chair, feeling a little more normal. The orderly made sure his feet and legs were properly supported. “Would you like me to take you for a walk?”

“Please,” Marty answered. He reached out and took his mother’s hand. “I need to try, Mom.” Marty saw her nod as the orderly wheeled him out of the room. His mother followed, and once they reached a wide, quiet area of hallway, the orderly stepped back and stood near his mother.

Marty sat in the middle of the hallway and easily placed his right hand on the right wheel. His left hand took a lot more concentration. He thought of the exercises he’d done in PT and squeezed his fingers around the wheel. Slowly he pushed forward. His right hand moved the wheel, but his left hand slid off, making him spin slightly. “Fuck,” Marty swore quietly before trying again. A few times, he managed to move himself forward slightly, but mostly he just went in slow circles. Marty heard his mother gasp softly every time he failed, and his own frustration began to rise. Maybe he’d never got out of here and would be at the mercy of his family for the rest of his life. That thought alone was enough to make him try again.

"Come on, honey, let's head back," his mother said, but Marty was determined to be able to move himself.

"Hi, Marty," a woman said as she walked in his direction. "Dr. Fielding said you were going to try to wheel yourself." He looked up from his left hand and saw the physical therapist, Kristen, walking toward him. "Remember what we talked about. You can't work your hand the way you used to. Those pathways in your brain are gone. We have to create new ones."

"Okay," Marty agreed.

"Let's go on down to therapy. We can work better there than in the hallway." Kristen turned back to the orderly and Marty's mother. "We'll be about an hour," she explained.

"I'll wait for you," Marty's mother said before turning and walking back toward his room. Marty waved at her as Kristen walked him toward the elevators. They didn't talk much until they were in the private therapy room.

"Dr. Fielding said you might need a bit of rescuing," Kristen told him as she put on the brakes of the chair. "He's a good man and a great doctor."

"Is he married?" Marty asked, and Kristen shook her head. "Do you like him?"

Kristen chuckled as she knelt next to the left side of the chair. "I don't have the right equipment to catch his eye, if you know what I mean." Kristen took his hand gently in hers. "And I believe you do." Marty tried to pull his hand away, but his feeble attempt fell short. "Hey, it's okay. I've seen how you look at Franklin whenever he's in here. Like I said, it's fine. I won't tell anyone." Franklin was one of the other therapists, and Marty had tried not to be obvious, but it was hard not to watch the lean attractive man with the grace of a dancer.

"Was I that obvious?" Marty asked. He'd never told anyone that he liked boys, and he'd thought he was pretty good at keeping it a secret.

"Nah," she told him with a smile and they got to work.

For the next hour they worked hard, and by the end of the session, Marty was able to use his arms to move the wheelchair a little bit. It was an improvement, and Kristen reminded him that progress came in little steps rather than big leaps. "But you are progressing," Kristen told him, "and once you master the chair and get strength in your arms, we'll start to teach you how to walk again." Now there was something to look forward to.

Chapter Two

ANOTHER week had gone by, and Marty had largely mastered the chair. He could move both arms, and even if his left was still much weaker, he'd gotten some of his movement back. Every time Dr. Fielding came by, Marty hoped he'd have some news for him, but he said nothing, and Marty knew it was getting closer and closer to the day he'd be going home. He could feed himself now and even transfer himself to the bathroom with a little help. Thank God, those catheters and diapers were a thing of the past. He could feed himself and get around pretty well. He still had some residual effects in his legs, but he and Kristen had been working on those, too, even if it was just leg exercises on the floor. She said he was getting stronger.

"Morning," Dr. Fielding said when he walked into Marty's room. Marty had been in the hospital nearly two and a half months now, and he was more than ready to see the outside of those walls. "How are you feeling?"

"Really good," Marty answered.

"It looks like you'll be leaving us tomorrow afternoon," Dr. Fielding told him, and Marty kept expecting the doctor to continue. "I'll be by this afternoon and I have a colleague from medical school who would like to take a look at you if that's okay?"

"Sure, whatever you need," Marty answered sulkily as he realized the fact that he would be going home and be under his mother's care until the day he died. That was an exaggeration and he knew it, but the exasperation he felt was just as intense. He'd really been hoping Dr. Fielding would come through for him, but then again, what had he been expecting? If he didn't want to move back home, then he needed to take matters into his own hands. Maybe he could go back to school. Marty sighed. He wasn't enrolled in any classes and he wouldn't be able to attend any again until fall, and then he'd have to retake the ones he hadn't finished. This whole thing really sucked.

"We'll see you tomorrow, then," the doctor said, and Marty smiled and nodded slowly. His situation wasn't the doctor's fault.

"Thanks. I appreciate everything you've done."

Dr. Fielding walked toward the door and stopped. "Most of the progress you've made is because of your own drive and efforts. Don't let anyone tell you any different. Coming back as far as you have from a stroke as severe as the one you had is nothing short of amazing. Yes, you're young and in good shape, but it's the drive from inside that's going to get you back where you were." The doctor left, and Marty smiled as he relaxed in bed before turning on the television. He'd always been driven to go after what he wanted. He got that from his father.

Elected three times by the good people of Wyoming to represent them in the US Senate, William Green was driven to get what he wanted. A trait Marty had inherited. It didn't hurt that Marty's father was also one of the wealthiest men in the state, but he believed first and foremost in helping others rather than lining his own pockets. Marty was proud of his father, even if he and Marty's mother were more than a little paranoid about their children.

Marty watched television for the rest of the evening, performing the exercises that Kristen had shown him while he lay in bed. When he got sleepy, Marty turned off the lights and television before going to sleep, telling himself that there were worse places he could be going than home to a huge ranch with servants and horses. All he really wanted to do was leave the hospital and go back to school so he could see his friends, attend classes, and lead his own life, away from the ever-watchful eyes of his mother and father. Like that was going to happen.

Marty woke in the morning excited about leaving the hospital. Yes, he was going home, but he told himself it wouldn't be for long and then he could go back to school and be on his own again. He'd already eaten his breakfast and gotten himself to the bathroom to clean up by the time Dr. Fielding arrived to check on him. He was followed by a large man in jeans, a white shirt, and a cowboy hat.

"Marty, this is Dakota—Dr. Holden. He and I went to medical school together, and he has a ranch out near Jackson."

"Pleased to meet you," Dakota said, extending his hand, which Marty shook from his chair.

"Paul tells me you're looking for a job," Dakota told him, and Marty looked at Dr. Fielding, who nodded. "Did you think you were getting a free ride? You aren't. Paul told me about your case and that you aren't particularly interested in going home." Dakota reached over for the remote and turned off the television. "Why not?"

"Um," Marty began, and then he quieted, taking a few seconds to get his thoughts together. "I'll be coddled at home within an inch of my life. If she had her way, my mother would have had me in a motorized wheelchair for months. I don't want to be stuck there. Do you have any idea what my family is like?"

"I know your father. Not very well, but I know him, and what your parents have been through. But that's not what I'm asking. Paul says you've probably been here weeks longer than you needed to at your parents' insistence, and that you can probably work as long as it's not too strenuous." Dakota turned to look at Dr. Fielding. "He also said that you've come as far as you have on drive and determination. I know you grew up on a ranch and understand the kind of work involved, so I'm offering you a job for the spring and summer."

"Really?" Marty asked, looking alternately at Dakota and Dr. Fielding.

"Yes, but remember it is a job. No one sits around and gets a free ride on my ranch. We have horses and cattle that need tending to. Wally's cats need to be fed and taken care of. I have my medical practice, and Wally has his veterinary practice, so we're very busy."

"I think I can feed cats," Marty said, "and I can do anything else you want me to. I don't plan to be in this chair for long."

Dakota sat on the edge of the bed, chuckling. "Wally's cats are lions, tigers, and, currently, a panther. You won't be taking care of them. I only mentioned it because we're all very busy, so if you're thinking this will be some sort of vacation or dude ranch, think again."

"I know what a ranch is like and I'll pull my weight," Marty said, extending his hand, and Dakota shook it. "So when do I start?"

"I'll be in town for a few more days before I head back. There's just one more thing you need to do: tell your parents and get your father's blessing." Dakota handed him a business card with his phone number on it. "I'll talk to you soon." Dakota left the room, and Marty stared at Dr. Fielding, wondering just how in hell he was going to get his father's blessing. It would be impossible.

Still in his chair, Marty began getting his things together so he could go home. His mother arrived a little while later, and she helped him get the last of his things gathered. Marty had called a few of the guys on the team to tell them he was going home, and just before lunch a bunch of them showed up, including Kyle.

"All of us got together and we got you something," Kyle said, pulling a basketball out of a shopping bag. "The entire team and all the coaches signed it." Marty choked up, but he tried his best not to show it.

"Thanks, guys," Marty said, taking the ball and then bumping hands with the six men who stood in his room, towering over his mother.

"We also got you this," Payton, one of the team guards, said, and he handed Marty a rolled-up jersey. "Everyone got together, and we decided to reserve your number for when you come back." Marty unfurled the shirt, and sure enough, it was his number, with his name embroidered above it.

Marty swallowed and didn't know what to say. "Thank you," was all he could muster.

"What's all this?" Dr. Fielding asked as he came into the room. "Looks like a basketball team." Marty introduced his doctor to all the guys. "Looks like you can leave as soon as we finish the paperwork," the doctor told him.

"Then we'd better go," Kyle said, and the guys began to filter out. "But we expect you to come back."

"I will," Marty promised, and Kyle smiled at him before leaving.

"The nurse will bring in some papers for you to sign, and then you'll be ready to go," Dr. Fielding said before extending his hand for Marty to shake. "You keep that determined attitude." Marty nodded, and Dr. Fielding acknowledged his mother and then left the room. The nurse brought the papers to be signed, and then they packed Marty's things and were on their way.

Marty said good-bye to everyone as he was wheeled out of the hospital. He transferred himself to the passenger seat of his mother's Lincoln, and the orderly packed his chair into the trunk. Once all his stuff was stowed in the backseat, she got in the car, and they began the drive out of Cheyenne toward home. Marty didn't talk much during the drive, his thoughts occupied with how he was going to explain to his father that he had a job and wasn't going to be staying at home. He knew his only chance was to talk to his father, because the minute his mother got wind of what he wanted, she'd slam the door closed so fast and hard the sound would shake the house.

"We made up one of the rooms on the main floor for you. I made arrangements for a hospital bed if you think you'll need one."

Marty didn't want her making any special arrangements. He didn't plan on being there for very long. "A regular bed is going to be fine. I've had enough of hospital beds to last me the rest of my life."

His mother chuckled softly. "I'll bet you have." It had been a while since he'd seen her smile. Mom was a worrier, Marty knew that, and it had only intensified after what had happened to Shane.

"Everything's going to be okay, Mom," he said, trying to reassure her. "I'm going to get stronger, and soon I'll be walking again."

"I'm just glad to have you home," his mother told him, and Marty's gut twisted slightly. He knew what he was going to ask when he saw his father would hurt her. She wanted her children home with her, where she could protect them. It had been that way for years now, but Marty needed to be on his own and truly test his wings. He'd needed to do that before he'd had the stroke, but now he needed it even more, if only to prove to himself that he could survive on his own without someone to stand guard for him against the world. Without a doubt, he knew his mother would do that, and Marty loved her for it, but it wasn't what he thought he needed right now.

His mother turned off the main road and down their private drive. She stopped at the gates and entered her code, and then waited for them to open before continuing on. Marty knew his mother felt safer with the security around the house, but it was false. Marty and his siblings had been climbing that gate for years. His mother waited for the gate to close before continuing down the drive and up to the large, sprawling, ranch-style home. The architect who'd designed it had meant for the house to blend in with the surrounding landscape, and most of the time it did, but in the Wyoming winter it easily stood out against the snow. His mother pulled up as close to the front as she could. Cassie and Josh rushed out of the house and opened his door, and Marty collected hugs from his younger brother and sister. Thankfully, both of them were still young enough to be demonstrative, which was wonderful. "We helped Mama set up your room," Cassie said with an excited grin.

"Don't worry, we didn't mess up your real one," his brother added.

"Let's get him inside before Marty catches cold," his mother said, and the kids began unloading the back of the car while one of the hands got out the wheelchair. Marty transferred himself to it with a bit of difficulty, wishing he and Kristen had practiced this in therapy, and then he was wheeled inside.

It took a while for him to get unpacked and settled. The kids were off in another part of the house, and his mother had finally left him alone after fussing over him for an hour. After leaving his room, Marty glided down the hallway to his father's office, just off the foyer. The door was closed, and Marty knocked and waited. The door opened, and his father stood in front of him with a grin. "Sorry I wasn't there to help bring you home," he said, stepping back so Marty could enter the spacious office. "I have been on the phone all day with a policy crisis of epic proportions. I was about to come find you." His dad leaned down and hugged him gently, but warmly. Two of his father's aides sat in chairs across from the desk, and with a nod from his dad, they got up and left through the other door to their workspaces.

"I know you're busy, but I need to talk to you," Marty began, gliding up to his father's conference table. He figured he might as well get this over with. If there was going to be yelling and screaming, he wanted it over and done with.

"What's on your mind?" His father settled in the chair across from him. "This looks serious," his father added with concern.

Marty took a deep breath. "I've received an offer for a job and I'd like to take it," Marty began.

His father looked stunned. "You just got out of the hospital, and you know your mother is looking forward to having you home."

Marty had practiced what he wanted to say in the car on the way home. "I know she is, and I know I just got out of the hospital. For that matter, I know I can't walk yet, but that's why I need to take this job. I need to know I can stand on my own two feet, even if I'm in a wheelchair for the rest of my life. I don't want to be dependent on you and Mom." Marty knew his father could understand that. Marty's father had stepped away from his own family back east and made his way to Wyoming, started the ranch, and parlayed that into many successful businesses.

"I know you do," his father said with a smile. "We're a lot alike that way. But can't you wait for a while? You mother is going to hit the roof if you try to leave."

"I know, and I understand why." Marty's gaze traveled to the picture of five-year-old Shane that hung on his father's wall. "But, Dad, I can't let your fear keep me from living the rest of my life."

His dad said nothing, his mouth hanging open. After a minute, he said, "Is that what we've been doing?"

"Dad, there are locked gates around our home. You have aides that are built like brick walls. At night, cars patrol the access roads. When was the last time that any of us were outside alone? Even on our own property? Yes, I understand why things are the way they are. Shane's loss hit all of us hard, you and Mom especially, I know that. But you can't stop the rest of us from exploring the world."

Marty saw rather than heard his father sigh. "So where is this job?"

"It's at a ranch near Jackson," Marty said, knowing he'd only cleared the first hurdle. "The owner is a friend of Dr. Fielding's. They went to medical school together, and he's willing to hire me for the spring and summer. His name is Dakota Holden, and he said that he knew you slightly. He also said that he would only give me the job with your blessing."

Marty's dad nodded and seemed a bit impressed. "I seem to remember him. We worked together on some water-rights issues a few years ago. Can't say as I agree with all his views, but Dakota Holden is a fighter and he impressed me as an honorable man who was willing to fight for the benefit of his community, not just himself. You say he's a doctor?"

"Dr. Fielding said they were in the same class," Marty explained, feeling more positive by the second.

"Do you have a phone number for Dr. Holden?" his father asked, and Marty nodded, pulling out the card Dakota had given him. His father reached for it, but Marty pulled the card back.

"I'll write it down for you," Marty said, and his father grinned. "Don't give up any information you don't have to," Marty explained, spouting one of his father's words of wisdom. Senator Green was a shrewd man—he'd had to be to survive eighteen years in the US Senate and be respected by both parties. *Concentrate on what's important and stay out of the fights that get you nowhere, or worse, labeled as the poster child for something you don't agree with*, had been another of his father's long-held views. His father had long described himself as a moderate Republican who believed in basic personal freedoms, even those freedoms that extended to people he didn't necessarily agree with. Those views had made him some enemies on occasion, but had also won him a great deal of respect for his integrity and general voice of reason.

"I'll call him," his father said, "but that's all I can promise. I firmly believe you need to take more time to recuperate. But you're also nineteen, and as an adult, maybe it's time to start making adult decisions." His father stood up and walked back to his desk. "Your mother is planning a special dinner to celebrate your coming home." The phone rang on his father's desk, and Marty knew his father had to get back to work. Pressing him would only get him a firm no, so Marty left the office as his father's aides returned.

Marty wheeled himself to his temporary bedroom and managed to shift himself onto the bed, looking around what had once been a first-floor sitting room. Some of his pictures of basketball stars had been moved in to decorate the walls, along with bits of his furniture. His mother had obviously taken steps to make him feel as comfortable as possible.

"Hi, Marty," Cassie said from his doorway before running into the room and jumping on the bed. She had a book with her. "I can read this all by myself." She settled next to him and opened the book before reading it to him. By the time she was finished, Marty was half asleep. In some ways, it was definitely good to be home.

And in some ways, it wasn't. His mother checked on him every fifteen minutes, he swore. "Why is Mommy coming in here all the time?" Cassie asked before sliding off the bed. She raced away and returned with another book as his mother was making yet another "check that Marty's still breathing" stop.

"Let your brother rest," she told Cassie, and Marty extended his hand.

"You can read to me some more," he told her, and Cassie climbed back up on the bed after checking to make sure Mommy wasn't mad. "I'm fine, Mom." Marty turned toward her and smiled.

"Do you need something to drink?"

"I can get it for him." Cassie said.

"I'm fine, and my little nurse here can help me if I need it," Marty said, squeezing his sister in a hug. She giggled, and the happy sound filled the room. They read books for a while, and then Josh came in with his Wii. After hooking it to the television, they all played video games until it was nearly time for dinner.

The kids left to wash up, and Marty got into his chair before cleaning up in the downstairs bathroom and then rolling into the dining room. "I'd like to talk to you after dinner," his father said seriously and then went into the dining room, lifting Cassie for a hug and then setting her in her chair.

His mother and the cook had indeed outdone themselves, and by the time dinner was over, Marty was stuffed to the gills. He'd spent most of the meal watching his father for signs of what he wanted, but from his serious tone, it most likely wasn't good news. Once they'd eaten dessert and everyone had told stories about what had happened while Marty was away, the kids helped clear the table, and Marty followed his father to his office. His dad closed the door.

"I spoke with Dr. Holden, and he assures me that the job he offered you is legit. He also admitted that he's doing this as a sort of favor for Dr. Fielding, but he stressed that you'll be expected to work like the other guys." Marty wasn't sure if this was good news or not. "I asked him what your duties would be, and he said part of it was to spend time with his father. It seems that Dakota's dad has had MS for a while and is spending too much time alone. He understands that you won't be able to lift things, but he expects you to assist with Mr. Holden's care and be at his side for much of the day. You'll also have light chores until you're stronger. Dr. Holden has assured me that you'll get all the physical therapy you can handle from the therapist in his office." The serious look on his father's face didn't budge an inch. "If this is what you want to do, then I'll support it." His father shook his head. "You're definitely my son. I wanted to make it on my own, too, and I didn't always take the easiest way to do it."

"Thanks, Dad," Marty replied, and he felt his father's hand on his shoulder.

"Now comes the hard part—telling your mother."

Marty agreed, but he couldn't help smiling.

TWO days later, Marty had his bags packed and was waiting in the foyer for Dakota to pick him up. As expected, his mother had nearly come unglued, but Marty's father had assured her that the job was just for the spring and summer, and that it would be good for Marty. "He needs to be on his own," his dad had said. But the battle royal that ensued had nearly brought down the house when Marty's mother found out that his dad had already given his blessing and that Marty was leaving in two days.

"Do you have everything?" Marty's mother asked as she fussed around him. It didn't matter how angry she'd been two days ago, she still fussed.

"Yes, and if I need anything I'll have you send it. It's not like I'm going to be on the other side of the country. You can drive down for a visit if you want," Marty said, trying to soothe her. The truth was that even though he'd asked for this and had accepted the offer, he was nervous. He really didn't have any idea what Dakota and his family were going to be like. He hoped he got along with everyone and that he wasn't getting in over his head. "I'll be in contact so I can sign up for my classes in the fall, and I promise I'll be back for some of the holidays and the summer barbeque if I possibly can."

His mother began to cry softly as a large truck pulled down the drive. "I'm going to miss you."

"I know, and I'm going to miss you, but I'll call you at least twice a week. I have my computer, so we can Skype, and I promise that if I hate it, I'll call and come home." The doorbell rang, and Marty's mother answered it.

"Morning, ma'am, I'm Dakota Holden."

His mother took the offered hand. "We met at a water-rights gathering."

"Yes, we did. I'm surprised you remember me." Dakota smiled and began picking up Marty's bags. "Excuse me, but we need to get going or we won't get there before dark."

Marty turned to his mother and she gave him a hug. The kids and his father had said their good-byes last night. The kids were already on their way to school, and his father had caught an early flight to Washington, so it was just them. "I'll take care of myself." She nodded but didn't say anything. "I love you," Marty said, setting his last bag on his lap and then rolling out of the house and out toward the truck. He needed a bit of help from Dakota to get into the truck, but soon he was waving to his mother through the window.

"There's no need to be nervous," Dakota said as they headed through town and out toward the highway.

"Who said I'm nervous?" Marty said, and Dakota chuckled.

"Of course you are," Dakota said. "You're going to a strange place with people you haven't met; of course you're nervous. But we have a great ranch, and I really think you're going to like it." Dakota continued driving, and they talked about the horses and cattle, what Marty would be doing, and some about the town. Eventually, Marty began to nod off, and Dakota kept driving, letting him sleep.

Marty woke when the road got rougher. "Sorry," Marty said.

"No problem," Dakota answered. They continued driving and went through a small town. Marty took in everything as they passed and then they headed back out into ranch country. Eventually they turned down a country road, and then, after a few miles, into a driveway. Dakota pulled the truck up to a normal-looking ranch house. As soon as he turned off the engine, all hell seemed to break loose. Dogs barked, and a small man hurried out of the house without a coat on. Snow flew as he raced to the truck, and as soon as Dakota stepped out of the truck, the man was in Dakota's arms… and they were kissing.

Marty's mouth fell open and he tried not to look, but he couldn't help himself. He'd never seen two men kiss like that before, and it was hot. Marty looked away but then turned his head back again as he heard them walking around the truck. "Marty," Dakota said as he pulled open the door, "this is Wally." Dakota was grinning, and Marty extended his hand.

"It's great to meet you," Marty said, still a bit shocked and excited, with a touch of *oh my God, where am I really?*, and he hoped he covered it well. Wally began pulling bags and suitcases out of the back and then carried them into the house while Dakota brought around his chair. The huge man lifted him into the chair, and for a second he was totally jealous of Wally. Dakota was a stunningly handsome man, and knowing he was gay seemed to arouse Marty's curiosity.

Once Marty was in the chair, Dakota pushed him through the slushy snow to the door, and after cleaning off the wheels, pushed him inside, where Marty took over. He wasn't expecting anyone to cater to him. Dakota had made it clear that when he took the job, he was to be as self-sufficient as possible. Even his father had told him to do everything he could for himself and to handle himself like a man.

Wally met him inside and led him through the immaculately clean and very masculine house. There were no frilly curtains or flowery fabrics. Instead, leather furniture and a huge television filled the living room, with photographs and paintings of horses on the walls. As they continued, Marty glanced into the open dining room, with its huge, rough-hewn table and large chairs. This was a house that appeared to have been built and designed for comfort, rather than show. His family's home had originally been built to impress, and it showed, but this was a house meant for living. Marty was struck by its comfort and warmth. "I've put you in the room next to Dakota's dad's," Wally told him, and Marty followed him down the hall. "It has a door wide enough for your chair, but it doesn't have its own bath. The one in the hall should be large enough for the chair, and for showers you can use the bathroom off Jefferson's room. It has everything you could need."

Marty hadn't thought of things like that, but it appeared Wally and Dakota certainly had. Wally pushed open the bedroom door and stepped back so Marty could roll inside.

"Wally," said a rather tall, nervous-looking young man as he approached. Marty turned around and caught himself looking the man over from head to toe. He'd had to train himself not to stare at other guys, but given Wally and Dakota, he figured it wouldn't hurt to have a look. "Mr. Jessup called, and he's got a colt that tangled in some barbed wire. He says it isn't too bad, but he asked if you'd come take a look to make sure it doesn't get infected."

"I'll go now and call him back on the way." Wally turned toward him. "Marty, this is Quinn Summers, he's my veterinary assistant. Best one in this part of the state." Marty smiled, and Quinn colored slightly at the compliment. "Would you help make sure Marty gets settled?"

"Of course," Quinn said, and Wally hurried away while Quinn stood shyly near the door. Marty's bags were on the bed, and he opened them, wondering where he was going to put his clothes. The dresser had three drawers he could use, but the top one was above his reach. "Do you need help?" Quinn asked quietly.

"Please. I haven't been in this chair very long and I'm not sure how to take care of some things," Marty explained. Quinn cautiously moved into the room and opened the closet door. "Dakota called yesterday and asked if I could put a lower rod in here for you," Quinn said, and Marty smiled when the saw the secondary rod hanging below the higher one.

"So you're more than Wally's assistant," Marty commented.

"Yeah. My dad's a carpenter, so I've been able to do basic repairs and things since I was a kid." Quinn reached up to the higher rod and pulled down some hangers, and Marty watched as Quinn's strong, lean body stretched. "Do you need help getting things hung up?"

"I should be able to manage," Marty said, and Quinn smiled before leaving the room. Marty watched him go and then turned his attention to the task at hand. This place was going to be one hell of a temptation, that was for sure. Marty had known he liked boys for a while. He'd figured it out when he was a young teenager, but he knew he couldn't be gay. It was something that just couldn't be. His father was not known for taking a particularly tough stance on social issues—he was known more for his fiscal policy—but he was a Republican, after all. And having a gay child was not going to endear him to the voters. He was pretty sure his father had no idea Wally and Dakota were gay, or he'd never have agreed to let him come work on the ranch. Marty knew his father was coming up for reelection again at the end of the year, and the last thing he needed was to have to choose between his son and his job. What if his father didn't choose him? No, Marty had to put out of his mind any notion of acting on his feelings, even if he was on a ranch owned by a gay couple. He'd taken this job to prove he could survive on his own, and by God, he was going to do it. Marty got busy putting his clothes away and getting settled.

Once he was done, Marty wheeled himself carefully through the quiet house. The door to the room they'd said Mr. Holden used was closed, so Marty went to sit in the living room, wondering what he should do.

"All unpacked?" Dakota asked as he poked his head in the front door, and Marty nodded. "Good. Get your coat, and I'll take you out to the barn. You can meet the horses and see some of what we do. When the weather is better, you'll have some chores out there."

"Really?" Marty was trying to figure out what he could do in the barn.

"Yes. You can water horses and fill mangers, sweep floors, and organize tack," Dakota explained. "Your dad said you have horse experience so I thought that would be a good fit."

Marty wheeled himself to his room, grabbed his coat off the bed, and then wheeled back. After shrugging on the coat as he squirmed in the chair, Marty was ready to go, and Dakota held the door as he wheeled himself onto the porch and down the ramp. "I'll help you across the snow if you need it," Dakota offered, letting Marty lead as he navigated across a packed path of compacted snow. It was more difficult than moving on regular floors, and Marty's left arm tired as he reached the barn, but he made it without Dakota's help. Inside the barn, horses poked their heads above stall doors, and Dakota handed Marty some carrots for treats. One of the horses nearest him stretched its neck, and Marty moved closer, stroking the long nose as he fed the horse a carrot. "You're a good one, aren't you?" Marty crooned in his horse-soothing voice.

"He'll do anything for a treat," Dakota said with a chuckle. A phone rang, and Dakota fished his out of his pocket. He listened to what the caller said. "Okay, I'll meet you at the office. I'm on my way." Dakota hung up the phone and started moving toward the barn door. "Can you get back to the house?"

"Sure," Marty answered quickly. He'd made it here fine, so he figured he could get back. He moved on to greet the next horse while Dakota hurried outside, and soon Marty heard Dakota leave in his truck. The barn was remarkably quiet and peaceful. Marty acquainted himself with each of the horses, quickly learning which ones were aggressive, shy, or totally affectionate. Of course, the treats helped, and Marty got lots of head bumps as the horses looked for more carrots. After meeting the horses, Marty located where everything was, and after making sure the horses had food and water, like Dakota had mentioned at the house, Marty decided it was time to head inside.

It was nearly fully dark by the time Marty left the barn, the outside light shining off the snow. He started back toward the house after sliding the barn door closed as best he could. The door was heavy, but it moved pretty well. Marty made a note to himself to ask someone to check it before nightfall just in case it wasn't closed all the way.

The snow crunched under his wheels as he made his way back toward the house. He got about halfway and wished he hadn't told Dakota he could make it back. His left arm ached and his right arm felt sore from trying to compensate, but he didn't give up. Marty stopped once to rest for a few minutes before continuing on. God, how stupid could he be? He wasn't up to full strength yet, and no matter how much he wished he were, he needed to understand his limitations. Marty was afraid that this was beyond him. The slight uphill grade was making returning to the house more difficult than the trip down to the barn.

He'd almost made it. Just another ten feet and he'd be at the ramp. Marty stopped to catch his breath and rest his arms, shifting slightly in the chair. And that was his mistake. The change in weight made the chair slide sideways, and then Marty was falling. He couldn't stop it, so he pulled his arms to his body as the chair continued tipping. Marty braced himself and ended up sprawled on his side in the snow, half out of the chair. He wasn't hurt, thank goodness, but no one seemed to be around. He listened, but only heard the soft sounds from the barn and the sound of the light wind. "Help!" Marty called a few times in case anyone could hear him, but it appeared that no one could.

Marty pulled himself away from the chair, using his good leg to prop himself up onto his knee. His legs were still weak, and it took a great deal of balance to keep from falling back into the snow. Marty tried to turn the chair upright, but the ground was slippery enough that he couldn't seem to get enough purchase, and the wheels tended to slide rather than tip back up. Marty couldn't remember feeling this helpless in his life. In the hospital, he'd had people around ready to help, and at home he had more help than he needed, but now he was damned near helpless, tired, and cold was seeping into his legs, making him shiver and even more unsteady.

"Marty," he heard someone call, and he looked up as Quinn raced toward him without a coat on. "Are you all right?" Quinn asked, but he didn't stop to wait for the answer. Quinn righted the chair and then lifted Marty into his arms, cradling him against his warm body. Marty held him tight as Quinn took the few steps to the chair and gently set him back in it. "You didn't get hurt, did you?"

"Only my pride," Marty retorted, knowing that if his mother found out about this she'd be on her way to pick him up in two seconds.

"Let's get you inside," Quinn said and began pushing the chair out of the snow and up the ramp. He held the door, and Marty wheeled himself inside. Never had he been so happy to feel warmth around him. His legs shook and ached from the cold. He hadn't been out there that long, but the cold and snow had very quickly soaked right through his clothing. Quinn helped him get his coat off and then wheeled him down the hall to his room. Marty pulled a pair of sweat pants and a thick shirt out of a drawer. After pulling off his wet shirt, he pulled on the dry one and then shimmied out of his pants. The wet fabric clung to his legs, and thankfully, Quinn helped pull them off. Marty saw Quinn looking at him nearly naked and felt himself turn red. Quinn seemed to do the same thing, and then turned away. As fast as he could, Marty shimmied around like he'd been taught in therapy and got his pants on.

Feeling much warmer and drier, Marty looked at the pile of wet clothes, and Quinn bent to pick them up. "I'll hang them in the laundry room to dry. It's just off the kitchen." Quinn hurried away, and Marty sighed as he remembered how it had felt for those few seconds when Quinn held him. Yes, he knew he shouldn't feel that way, and he had no intention of acting on his feelings, but it was nice to remember.

"Did something happen?" Wally asked, stopping in the doorway.

"I had a little trouble getting back from the barn," Marty admitted, but he didn't want to make too much of it. "Quinn helped me, and I'm fine now." Marty didn't know quite what to do about the unsettled feelings that kept coming to mind whenever he thought of Quinn. Marty turned away, and Wally walked into the room and sat on the edge of the bed.

"I know this is very different for you. But part of the reason that Dakota agreed to have you come work here is because… well… he wanted you to have a chance to be yourself—your whole self." Wally looked at him intently, and Marty involuntarily looked down at his legs. "Dr. Fielding and a number of people at the hospital all think the world of you, and that's why Dr. Fielding contacted Dakota. They've all spent months with you and they know you have decisions to make and things about yourself that you need to sort out and come to terms with." Wally looked at him as though he could see the secrets of Marty's heart.

"You know?"

Wally smiled and nodded once.

"How? Did someone tell you?" Marty asked, shaking a bit.

"No one told us, because no one had to. And no, you don't come across as swishy or anything. Dakota just has a very keen sense of gaydar and when someone is hurting either on the outside or on the inside. It's what makes him a good doctor." Wally paused and Marty tried to process what he'd just been told. "But here, it doesn't matter. So you'll be free to come to terms with who you are."

"But it does matter. I can't be gay, I just can't. I know you and Dakota are happy, I saw that the minute you two were together, but it would hurt my family. You know who my father is, so you know how my being gay would hurt him." Marty earnestly looked into Wally's eyes, hoping he'd have some answer Marty hadn't thought of.

"Whatever you decide is fine. But think about this: you are gay. You can accept it or try to bury it, but I can guarantee, being gay is part of who you are, so it won't stay buried, no matter how much you may want it to." Wally stood up and lightly squeezed Marty's shoulder. "Dinner will be in half an hour, and afterwards you can meet Jefferson." Wally left the room, leaving Marty with a great deal to think about.

Chapter Three

"I HAVE to go to work, Dad," Quinn said as he got ready to leave their small place just outside of town.

His father scoffed as he shuffled through the house toward the bathroom. "Don't know why you have to work there. Those people aren't right."

"Because they're gay?" Quinn challenged. This had been the almost constant refrain since he'd taken the job as Wally's veterinary assistant.

"People are going to think you're gay too," he added, and Quinn bit his lip to keep from blurting out that he was. Instead, he kept quiet, like he always did. His father was in deep denial, and they both knew it. He and his father had talked about this a number of years ago, once, and then, at his father's insistence, the subject had never been discussed again. Quinn knew what his father really meant was that he didn't care if his son was gay as long as no one knew about it.

"You know, you'd think you'd be nicer since Wally saved Duchess for you when she was foaling a few months ago. So instead of burying a horse in the dead of winter, you have a mother and foal in the paddock. Think about that the next time you want to badmouth someone."

"Don't sass me," his father retorted as he closed the bathroom door.

"Pointing out your closed-mindedness isn't sass; it's telling the truth," Quinn said loudly through the bathroom door before walking away. “Sometimes you’re an old fool.” There were days when he wondered why he didn’t take Wally and Dakota up on their offer to move into the bunkhouse on the ranch. There was room, and some days Quinn was sorely tempted. “I’m leaving,” he called through the house before walking outside into the cold, early spring morning. Quinn wrapped his coat around himself and hurried to his truck, starting it fast and then heading out for the ten-minute drive to Wally’s.

The trip was normal, and as he pulled into the drive, he saw Liam heading out of the barn, trudging through the remaining snow to the pens behind the house where Wally kept his big cats. Quinn usually stayed away and let Wally and Liam handle them—they weren’t his cup of tea—although during the summer one of the lions had injured a paw and Wally had tranquilized him. Quinn had assisted with the minor surgery, and it had been pretty amazing to be that close to an adult male lion. But that was the only way he wanted to be that close. After parking the truck, he got out, went inside the house, and found Wally with Marty in the living room.

Quinn smiled at the other man and he saw Marty smile back. Quinn found the younger man enthralling, and he’d hoped Marty would warm up after being at the ranch a while, but he’d been a bit distant to Quinn the few times he’d seen Marty in the barn. Quinn had asked Dakota about it, and all he’d gotten was a “give him time.”

“I need to go sit with Jefferson,” Marty said, and he rolled down the hall. Quinn watched him go and turned to Wally with a soft sigh. Many times over the past few weeks, Quinn had thought Marty simply wasn’t interested, and he could live with that. But every now and then he’d walk into the room and Marty would smile at him. Not a practiced smile, but a genuine one that reached all the way to his blue eyes, and Quinn’s heart would jump at the sheer innocent beauty in the simple gesture. For a while he’d thought that Marty was shy, but he wasn’t. Marty was outgoing with everyone but him. He'd also thought that Marty might have been embarrassed because Quinn had seen him nearly naked, but the more he watched him, he didn't think that was it, either. The only conclusion he could come to was that Marty didn't find him interesting enough. Quinn knew Marty came from a wealthy family and that his dad was Senator Green. He figured Marty had probably met all kinds of interesting, clever people and that he simply didn't measure up.

"Are you going to sit down, or stare at the table?" Wally said with an impish smile.

"What's wrong with me?" Quinn asked absently, his thoughts still on Marty as he sat down to review the day's appointments.

"Nothing," Wally said. "You need to give him time."

"That's what Dakota said, but maybe it's not time—maybe it's me." Quinn pulled his attention to the task at hand just as Wally closed the appointment book.

"You've got it bad, haven't you?" Wally asked, and Quinn hesitated before nodding slowly. "You need to let him work things out at his own pace. He's coming to terms with who he is, and we all need to give him a little space. Besides," Wally said as he leaned closer, "if you saw the looks he gives you when you aren't looking, you wouldn't be worrying whether anything was wrong with you. But I will tell you this: if you're interested, truly interested, maybe you should try saying something instead of mooning over him all the time. He isn't sure of himself in the love department, and he's probably scared of being rejected."

"You mean like ask him on a date?"

"Ding, ding, ding," Wally teased. "That's where people usually start. So, see what he likes to do and take him there. Talk to him instead of trading enigmatic smiles and goo-goo-eyed gestures." Wally opened the appointment book. "Now, let's get down to business."

They talked for about half an hour and then walked outside and around to the back of the barn, where Dakota had built a clinic for Wally. It wasn't very large, but it was neat and it served their purposes, since Quinn and Wally mostly went to their patients. Quinn helped Wally load the truck with supplies, and then they got in and started the day's appointments.

He and Wally were gone most of the day. When they got back, Quinn carried the supplies they no longer needed back to the clinic, passing Marty as he was checking the mangers for water and hay. He hurried past, giving Marty a quick smile, and got everything put away. By the time he was done, Marty was nowhere to be found in the barn, so Quinn walked across the slushy yard and found Marty working with Wally in the kitchen.

"I need to get some things from the cellar. Could you watch the soup for me?" Wally asked Marty and then hurried away and down the stairs. Quinn shook his head when Marty wasn't looking, knowing Wally had purposely left the room. Quinn knew that Wally was a notorious matchmaker. The man was always trying to fix people up, with very mixed success.

"So, Marty, do you like it here?" Quinn knew it was pretty lame, but he didn't know quite how to start a conversation with Marty. "How's Mr. Holden doing?" Quinn asked.

"He seems…." Marty turned around, and Quinn saw sadness in his eyes. "He's so tired all the time. When he's awake, he's one of the nicest people I've ever met."

"Dakota's dad is pretty special," Quinn agreed. "Has he told you some of his stories yet?"

Marty shook his head slowly. "He doesn't seem very talkative," Marty answered, reaching up to stir the soup. The pot was a little high for Marty, so Quinn stepped in to help, stirring the rich-smelling concoction with a wooden spoon. Speaking of not very talkative, Quinn waited for Marty to continue, but he stayed quiet.

"The ranch here must be pretty different from what you're used to," Quinn commented, and Marty nodded, but didn't say anything. Having a conversation was like pulling teeth. "What's your home like?"

"It's just a home," Marty answered.

"It must be fascinating to have a father who's a senator. Have you ever been to Washington and seen him in action?" Quinn asked, and he saw a spark of interest in Marty's face that quickly faded again.

"Once, when I was a kid, the whole family went to Washington and Dad took us to the Capitol. I remember holding Shane as the two of us gazed up at the dome. He laughed and stretched his little arms, trying to reach the ceiling, and then laughed some more when he realized how high up it was." Marty smiled, and Quinn breathed a sigh of relief that he might have found a subject that Marty wanted to talk about, but the other man quieted again.

"Is Shane your brother?" Quinn asked.

"Yes." Marty glided away, leaving the room, and Quinn wondered what the hell had just happened. The last thing he'd wanted was for Marty to leave, but now he was standing alone in the kitchen stirring soup for Wally. *Way to make use of the opportunity.* Quinn heard Wally's footsteps on the stairs, and when Wally came into the kitchen, Quinn shrugged and handed over soup duty to Wally before wandering down the hall. He found Marty in his room, the door open. Quinn stepped inside, and Marty showed Quinn a picture. "I didn't mean to run away."

The picture showed a happy family, all six of them smiling. Quinn could easily pick out a teenage Marty standing next to his father. "Where was this taken?" Quinn sat on the edge of the bed.

"The Speaker of the House was a friend of my dad's, so he took us through the chambers, and since Congress wasn't in session at the moment, he had Josh sit in his chair, and the rest of us gathered around for a picture." Marty pointed to the little girl in her mother's arms. "That's my sister, Cassie. She was three in this picture. Of course, that's my mom and dad; Josh was nine, and I was fourteen. My father is holding Shane. He was six when this was taken. He'd be eleven now."

"What happened to him?" Quinn asked softly, and Marty turned to him.

"He was kidnapped a month after this picture was taken. Someone came on the property and took him right out of the front yard. I can remember my mother looking for him frantically, but she never found him. There was no ransom demand or anything." Quinn thought Marty's voice remained remarkably steady. "They caught the guy when he was trying to snatch another kid a week later, and during questioning, he told them where to find the rest of the bodies. One of them was Shane's." Marty lifted his gaze. "I was supposed to be watching him, but I'd gone inside to get him a juice box, and when I came out again, he was gone. At first I thought he was playing hide-and-seek."

Quinn felt his mouth hang open. "It wasn't your fault."

"I know that now. My parents told me the same thing, and once the shock and grief began to wear off for all of us, they found a counselor who helped me realize that the kidnapper probably would have taken me too, or had simply been waiting for an opportunity. We'll never know. After he told them where the bodies were, he hung himself in his cell. So we'll never know anything more." Marty shrugged, and then, reaching up, he set the picture on the dresser.

"I wanted to ask you something, but maybe now isn't a good time," Quinn thought out loud, and then he realized what he'd done. He figured he might as well ask, because it wasn't fair to say something like that and then leave. "I was wondering if you'd like to go to the movies with me on Saturday? There are a couple of films we can choose from, and the theater is sort of interesting.

It's one of those old movie houses, but it was converted to a relatively modern theater a few years ago."

Marty didn't answer right away, and Quinn thought that he was going to be turned down. "That would be nice." Marty sounded skeptical, but Quinn took the acceptance at face value.

"Great, it should be fun," Quinn said, standing up. "I'd better see if Wally needs anything before I go home." Quinn headed back into the kitchen. Wally was setting the table, and when Marty joined them, he pitched in. After checking in with Wally, Quinn said good-bye, sharing a smile with Marty before pulling on his coat. "Call me if something comes up," he told Wally, who promised he would, and then Quinn headed out to his truck and drove home.

His father was sitting in the living room, drinking what looked like his third beer, when Quinn walked in. "How was work?" Quinn asked as he breezed through the room.

"The usual." His father drained the last of his bottle and set it on the coffee table. "I thought you might be eating there," he commented, getting up from his chair. "You seem to be spending a lot of extra time with them."

"I know we haven't talked about this much, but you know I'm gay," Quinn began.

"Yeah, but the rest of the world don't need to know it," his father retorted. "What is everyone going to say?" Quinn's father walked toward the kitchen, probably to get another beer. He drank too much, Quinn knew that, but thankfully, it only seemed to be in the evenings. Instead of opening the refrigerator, his dad pulled open one of the cabinets and pulled out a box of cheap mac and cheese. Damn, if that was what his dad was making for dinner, Quinn wished he'd stayed at Wally and Dakota's. Quinn pulled open the refrigerator door, but there wasn't much inside, and the cabinets were probably equally bare. It was definitely time for him to move out and find a place of his own. Moving into the bunkhouse was looking more and more preferable by the day.

"They're probably going to say that you have a son to be proud of. Wally and I have helped all of them more than once, and they aren't too proud to accept the help, so you'd think they'd be man enough to accept that not everyone is like them." Quinn left the kitchen to let his father make what he wanted and went down the hall to his room. After he took off his work clothes, Quinn showered and dressed, figuring he'd head into town for some dinner. "I'll see you later," he told his dad as he walked through the house, stopping just long enough to grab his coat before making a beeline to his truck. He'd just pulled out of the drive when his phone rang. Quinn answered, putting it on hands-free.

"Quinn, it's Wally. Could you come back to the ranch? Kiley just called, and he has a horse that went missing. They found her, but she'd been attacked. I'm sorry to bother you, but I'm going to need some help."

"I'm on my way," Quinn said and pulled off the road, doing a three-point turn before racing out toward the ranch. Quinn parked and saw Wally in his truck. He jumped in, and the two of them took off. The drive wasn't far, and they pulled into the familiar ranch and got out, then hurried into the barn. They were met by Mr. Kiley, who simply shook his head.

"She was too far gone," he said quietly. "I called before I realized how bad it was. I had to put her down. She could barely breathe and was bleeding bad." Wally looked the way Quinn felt. When they lost an animal, Wally always felt like he could have done more. It was one of the things Quinn admired most about him.

"Do you know what attacked her?"

"Coyote. The winter's been so hard, and she was on her own. They didn't take her down, which was why I thought we could save her, but once I got her back, I realized she'd lost too much blood." Kiley sighed. It was part of life out here. "Can I offer you something to eat or drink for your trouble?"

"It's all right. We'll head back. Thank you anyway." Wally headed back toward the truck, and Quinn followed. Neither of them said anything on the ride back to the ranch. They got out and moved any perishable supplies to the clinic. "Come on inside. I think we could both use some food," Wally said.

Quinn went inside, and Wally motioned him into the living area, where Quinn found Dakota and Marty sitting with Dakota's dad. "Mr. Holden, how are you?"

"As well as could be expected," he answered, his speech slightly slurred. Quinn sat down near Marty's chair.

"Was everything okay?" Marty asked, and Quinn shook his head.

"The horse was hurt too badly. She was put down before we got there," Quinn answered before turning his attention to the television. "Dakota, is your offer to move to the bunkhouse still open?"

Dakota looked surprised, but he nodded. "Of course. Is something wrong?"

"No more than usual," he answered before settling back on the sofa. Quinn felt Marty's gaze on him, and he turned to see the quizzical look on Marty's face. "How do I describe the relationship I have with my father?" Quinn whispered so he wasn't talking over the television. "My dad knows I'm gay, but would prefer that no one else know that Lyle Knepper has a gay son, if you know what I mean. He's more worried about what other people will think than anything else. There's nothing for me there anymore, anyway. It was just a place to live."

"Besides, you're here more than you're home," Wally said from behind him, handing over a bowl of soup. Quinn hadn't been aware that anyone other than Marty could hear him. "And we'd be happy to have you, you know that," Wally added. "More people have been through the rooms of this house in the last few years. So think about it, particularly if your dad's making trouble again. Maybe if you aren't there to help him with his chores and take care of things around the house, he'll learn to appreciate what he had." Wally sat on the arm of Dakota's chair, and Quinn watched as Dakota wound his arm around Wally's waist. The simple gesture was surprisingly intimate, especially when Wally leaned closer as he ate. Occasionally Dakota would turn away from the television just to glance at Wally, and the expression on his face was one Quinn had seen many times and had come to call their "look of love," because anyone who saw it knew exactly what it meant. Those two people completed each other and were only truly, blissfully happy around the other.

Quinn looked away because he felt like a bit of a voyeur and saw Marty watching them as well, with a bit of a questioning look on his face. He gave Marty a small smile and then turned his attention back to the television and to the soup Wally had brought him. When he was done, Quinn took the dishes to the kitchen, and when he returned, Wally had shifted and was half sitting on Dakota's lap, being hugged like he was the most precious thing in the world. And Quinn had no doubt that, to Dakota, Wally was exactly that.

Quinn wanted to have that kind of devotion in his life, someone who would love him above everyone else. He thought he'd had that, once. But it wasn't to be. Well, actually, Quinn knew he'd simply hung his hat on the wrong man. He knew that now, but at the time… it hadn't been pretty.

"What's your dad like?" Marty asked.

"Typical, I guess," Quinn answered with a small sigh as he turned to face Marty, making sure to keep his voice low. "I told my dad quite a while ago that I was gay. I wasn't even twenty and I really expected him to kick me out of the house, ya know. But he didn't. Dad sort of shrugged and told me that stuff like that was no one else's business and that it should stay that way. At the time I thought he was being kind of supportive, but now I realize it was his way of burying his head in the sand. Sort of like, if nobody else knows about it, then he won't have to deal with it either and can go on as though nothing changed. That's my dad all over." Quinn scoffed lightly. "Sometimes it's like I was raised by a teenager. It never seemed to matter what I thought or even what he thinks. It's all about what his friends think, and they're not exactly rocket scientists."

"You can say that again," Wally commented as Dakota held him a little tighter, shushing him lightly as Jefferson began to get agitated because he couldn't hear the television.

"Do you want me to take you to your room?" Dakota asked, and his father scowled at him—or at least as close to a scowl as he could manage. Quinn had seen Mr. Holden getting a little worse each day. Thankfully, he was still with it and could still see and hear. His body was just giving out on him. It made Quinn sad, because he remembered the energetic and fun Mr. Holden from when Quinn was a kid. Quinn used to wish sometimes that Mr. Holden had been his dad.

"Wanna watch the game," he said softly, his voice barely understandable.

The action in the basketball game began again, and Quinn saw Marty's attention shift back to it. He did the same, and they all sat quietly until the game had ended. Then Dakota wheeled his father down the hall to his room, and Quinn helped Wally clean up the room before sitting on the end of the sofa nearest Marty.

"Are you really going to move here?" Marty asked, and Quinn hedged rather than committing.

"I'm thinking about it really seriously. Dad isn't making things easy, and he seems to just want me to take care of him,"

Quinn answered. "The truth is, I'm not very happy there, and I feel at home here."

"Then that's good," Marty told him but didn't say much more. "You should be where you feel comfortable."

"I take it you aren't right now," Quinn said as he watched Marty squirm slightly in his chair. "It's okay if you're not."

Marty shrugged. "I guess I've had a bunch of things to think about." He looked over to where Wally and Dakota had been sitting. "I always thought the fact I was gay was something I'd have to hide for the rest of my life."

"You don't sound convinced that you don't," Quinn said, and Marty's expression became as serious and intense as a heart attack.

"I don't know how I feel," Marty admitted, and Quinn smiled slightly. He'd gone through a similar period of self-doubt when he'd begun the process of coming out and accepting who he was.

"You don't have to decide everything all at once. Take it one step at a time, and as long as you're honest with yourself, you'll find your way."

Wally came back into the room. "Quinn, you're welcome to stay here for tonight if you want," he offered, and Quinn accepted and thanked him. Wally left the room and returned a little later with a sheet and some blankets for the sofa. "I'll see you in the morning." Wally left the room again, leaving him and Marty alone. He looked at Marty, trying to think of something to ask him.

"How's therapy progressing?" He'd seen Marty going to what Wally had said were therapy appointments for the past two weeks. He'd avoided talking about Marty being in a chair or how he got there for fear it was something Marty didn't want to talk about, but he was getting a bit desperate.

"Pretty well. We're working to strengthen my arms a little more, and then the therapist says we'll start working to teach me how to walk again." Marty seemed excited, and the nervousness Quinn had felt about bringing up the subject fell away. "Before my stroke, I played basketball, so I had great muscle tone, but months in the hospital and the fact that my nerve paths are kind of shot mean that I've lost a lot of my strength. The therapist says I should have an easier time than most people, but they don't really know for sure."

"So you will be able to walk again," Quinn said, and Marty nodded.

"I want to be able to play basketball again." Marty sounded really determined, but the fear in his eyes betrayed his real feelings, complete with doubt.

"Then you will," Quinn said before Marty could express the doubt and fear that seemed to Quinn to be so very close to the surface. "You can accomplish anything you put your mind to. I want to become a veterinarian, like Wally, but I have to get the money together so I can go back to school. I got some so I could be a veterinary assistant, but…." Quinn let his voice trail off.

"What happened?"

"My dad got hurt, and I had to return to the ranch to take care of things," Quinn answered quickly. Marty's eyes narrowed slightly, like he could sense Quinn's evasion, but thankfully he didn't call him on it. What he'd said was the truth, just not the whole story. "Once I returned, I was lucky enough to get the job with Wally, and I absolutely love it. I'd like to do more, and someday I will, but right now I need to save some money."

"Have you always been around animals?" Marty asked.

"Yeah. Dad works as a carpenter, and we have a small place closer to town. We raise a few horses to sell for riding and things like that, nothing as big as what Wally and Dakota have. Did you grow up around horses too?"

"Oh yeah. My mom used to say she was never sure which I loved more, basketball or horses." Marty looked down at his legs. "Now I can't really do much with either." Marty paused for a moment, but when he lifted his eyes, that determined look was back. "I want to be able to do both again. Not necessarily at the same time, but…."

"Wouldn't it be great if we could figure out how to do both at the same time?" Quinn laughed. "Can you imagine the dribbling?"

"From the players and the horses," Marty added as he began to laugh.

"Charging up the court would be a whole new experience," Quinn added, and Marty's laughter increased. "Maybe we'd offer points if the horse stopped short and the rider was catapulted into the basket."

"We'd have to award those to the horse," Marty quipped, and Quinn laughed harder. Marty glowed when he laughed, the care that seemed to etch his face most of the time slipping away in the unguarded moment. It was nice to see. Slowly their laughter died away, and Marty looked around them. The rest of the house was dark and quiet. "I think everyone's in bed." Marty released the brakes on his chair. "I probably should be going too." Marty backed away and began wheeling himself toward the hallway. "I'll see you in the morning."

"Okay," Quinn said, watching as Marty disappeared from sight. After getting the bedding Wally had brought, he made up the couch and then quietly walked down the hall to the bathroom. He cleaned up as best he could and then returned to the living room. After undressing, he climbed into his temporary bed and turned out the light. He could hear the soft sounds of movement from the back of the house and he wondered if that was Marty getting undressed. If he thought the advance would be welcomed, he'd tiptoe down the hall and knock on Marty's door. God, he had it bad, and he knew he had to get his impulsive feelings under control. He'd acted on them before and had gotten his heart shattered. It was best to take Wally's advice and give Marty time. They had a date tomorrow, and Marty was still trying to figure out who he was. Quinn knew rushing him wasn't good, but damn, when he'd been laughing, Marty's happiness had seemed decadently addictive. Quinn played that moment in his mind over and over as his cock throbbed beneath the covers. For the millionth time, Quinn wondered why he always wanted what he couldn't have. "We have a date tomorrow," Quinn said to himself, and that brought a smile to his face and helped instill some patience. Closing his eyes, he willed his body to cooperate so he could get to sleep.

THE following afternoon, after Quinn and Wally had finished up their work, Wally shooed him home to get ready for his date. "Go get cleaned up—you smell like horse. And while there are worse things, no one wants to kiss someone who smells like a stable." Wally had grinned, and Quinn didn't have to be told twice. Hopefully, if he got home early, his dad would still be at work and he wouldn't get the third degree. As he approached the house, he saw that luck wasn't with him. After pulling his truck in next to his dad's, Quinn went inside. His father was nowhere to be found, so Quinn figured he must be in the barn. Not wanting to provide explanations about his plans for the evening, he showered right away and put on nice clothes and some cologne he'd had for a while, but it still smelled good, so he used a little before looking at himself in the mirror.

"Where are you going?" his father asked rather snarkily from the doorway. Quinn had been so intent on his task he hadn't heard his father come in the house.

"Out to the movies," he answered vaguely, opening his closet to find his nice jacket.

"Looks like you're dressed for a date to me," his father observed, and Quinn found the jacket he was looking for and grabbed his wallet and keys off the dresser before turning to face his dad.

"I'll see you later," Quinn said, hurrying by his dad, getting a good whiff of beer and horses on him. He heard his father follow him down the hall, but he stopped in the living room, and Quinn continued outside. He was about to leave when he decided to check things in the barn. The horses had water, but Mary Jane didn't have enough hay, so he added some to her manger. After seeing one of his father's half-assed efforts with the horses, Quinn took a few minutes to make sure every horse was settled before leaving the barn. Sometimes he really wondered who the adult was in their family.

Quinn carefully walked across the muddy yard, not wanting to get his shoes dirty, and got to his truck before heading out to pick up his date. As he drove, he should have been thinking about the time he was going to spend with Marty, but his thoughts centered around what he was going to do with the animals if and when he left home. His father was totally irresponsible. He could probably bring his own horses and other animals with him, but his father's horses would probably keel over from either thirst or starvation without Quinn to look after them. He pulled into the drive at Wally and Dakota's and parked as close to the house as he could. Quinn opened his door and was about to go inside when Marty rolled out onto the porch and then down the ramp.

"Do you need help getting in?" Quinn asked, already walking around to the passenger side.

"If you don't mind," Marty answered, and Quinn's heart did a little skip as he opened the door and carefully lifted Marty into his arms, and then placed him on the seat. He loved the way

Marty wound his arms around his neck and he thought of moving slower so they could stay that way a little longer. Once Marty was inside, Quinn moved his chair out of the way and closed the door. Quinn folded the chair and set it in the back, making sure it wouldn't move around before getting inside.

The ride to town was pleasant in the twilight. "What are we going to see?" Marty asked.

"I was hoping we could watch the new Willie Meadows movie, *Walking Away From Me,* but if you aren't into cowboy movies, we can see something else."

"I wanted to see that too," Marty answered with a grin. "I saw the commercials for it when I was in the hospital and I'd hoped I could see it, but then I came here. Between helping at the ranch and therapy, they keep me pretty busy." Marty looked out the windows as they rode. "I heard that Willie Meadows is gay and that he wrote the original song that they made into the movie for his boyfriend."

"I heard that too," Quinn said, and Marty looked and saw the huge grin on his face.

"What's so funny?"

"The boyfriend's name is Steve, and he's a really nice guy. He and Willie live a few miles from the ranch. Wally takes care of his horses, so I've been to their place a few times, and they always come to Wally and Dakota's summer barbeque." Quinn was really excited. "Are you a fan?"

"Sort of, I guess. I mean, I've read some stuff about him, and I like his music, but if I met him I wouldn't run up to him screaming or anything." Marty flashed a crooked grin that was completely adorable. "But it would be nice to meet him." Quinn nodded and kept his excitement to himself as best he could.

After he parked the truck near the theater, Quinn helped Marty out and into his chair, then walked next to him down the sidewalk to the box office. Quinn bought the tickets and made sure they had a place where Marty could sit. Then they went inside, and Quinn motioned Marty to the snack counter. "Order whatever you like."

Marty got a large popcorn and a soda while Quinn got M&Ms, licorice, and a soda. Then they made their way into the theater. Quinn gave Marty his snacks to hold and then held the back of Marty's chair as they went down the incline toward the front of the theater. It turned out that there were places especially for people in wheelchairs, and Quinn sat next to Marty as the previews began to play. "Five," Quinn said, and Marty looked at him, totally confused. "How many previews will they show? I say five."

"Oh, okay, four," Marty said. "What do I get if I'm right?"

"What do you want?" Quinn asked a little mischievously.

Marty seemed to think for a second. "I'll let you know if I win." He settled back, and as the previews played, Quinn could hear Marty counting. After four, the movie began to play, and Marty turned to him and grinned, then tossed a handful of popcorn into his mouth. The opening credits began, and they both turned their attention to the screen.

The movie had plenty of action, and Willie Meadows spent much of his time on screen looking larger than life. Quinn had indeed met him, but watching the movie, he fell under the spell of the story and the music that wound through the story of a cowboy who gets discovered and leaves home only to return and find that he had what he really wanted all along. The only disappointment was that the love interest was a woman. Quinn would have loved it if they had used a man, but this was no *Brokeback Mountain*. Still, the movie was great, and from what he'd heard people say, Quinn thought that Willie might have single-handedly resurrected a genre most people thought long dead—the singing cowboy. When Willie got the girl in the end, Quinn thought he might have heard a sniffle out of his companion, but he said nothing about it when the lights came up.

"That was really fun," Marty said as they headed up the aisle at the end of the line of people. "I can't believe he wrote all that music for another man."

"Love is love, Marty," Quinn said. "It doesn't mean it's any less intense or important simply because the feelings are between two men or two women." Quinn continued up the aisle, and they exited the theater. The air was still cold, with a few flakes of snow drifting from the sky. "Are you hungry? There's a little restaurant just down the way." Quinn motioned, and Marty moved ahead of him.

"You meant this to be a real date, didn't you?" Marty asked, and Quinn paused for a second.

"Of course I did," Quinn answered with a slight sigh.

"I meant, I guess I thought that guys would just fall into bed with one another, not go out on dates like…."

"Regular people," he finished, and Marty looked away.

"I didn't mean it like that. I guess I'd always heard things, and, well, I thought…." Marty swallowed and stopped moving. "I guess I thought it was only about sex."

"It's not," Quinn said, reaching out to take Marty's hand. "You saw Wally and Dakota last night, and how close they were. There's a lot more to their relationship than just sex. They manage the ranch, have their own businesses, take care of Jefferson, and somehow they even manage to make the lives of the people and even the animals around them better. That doesn't happen if a relationship is just based on sex." Quinn knew he was probably being a little more adamant than necessary, but he wanted a relationship, and he liked Marty. Quinn desperately wanted what Wally and Dakota had, but as he stood and looked at Marty, he realized he was probably getting ahead of himself once again. Marty was probably nineteen or twenty, and he was twenty-six. Those years translated to quite a difference between them.

Quinn had little doubt that Marty would eventually figure out who he was and what he wanted. Most people did. What he was really worried about was what Marty would want once he did. Most guys spent months sampling from the buffet of men that seemed to be around. Quinn had done that a little—after all, he lived in small-town Wyoming. Just how much was there to sample?

"You're far away," Marty said, and Quinn brought his attention out of his thoughts as they continued down the sidewalk.

"Sorry," Quinn replied with a small sigh. They reached the restaurant, and Quinn held the door open, letting Marty glide inside before following. He gave his name to the hostess, and she led them through the restaurant to a table where two other people were waiting.

"Who are they?" Marty asked quietly before turning back as the two people stood up. Quinn heard a gasp and knew the second Marty recognized one of the men at the table. "You're…."

"Wilson, and this is Steve," Willie Meadows said as he extended his hand.

"This is Marty," Quinn said before shaking hands with Wilson and Steve. The hostess took away one of the chairs, and Marty glided to the table. "We just came from the theater."

"The movie was great," Marty interjected, and both Wilson and Steve smiled. "Is it true you wrote the songs for Steve?"

Wilson nodded, smiling at the man sitting next to him. "I seem to write everything thinking of Steve. I'm working on a new album of material, and it's all cowboy love songs, some old, but most original."

"Were you upset that they made your love interest in the movie a woman?" Marty asked Quinn's question before he could.

"Wilson and I talked about it," Steve answered while Wilson drank from his water glass. "And we figured that the more successful the movie was, the better it was to show that Wilson being gay didn't matter to most people."

"Come on, Steve," Wilson chided.

"Okay. I hated it at first, because they were taking a song about me and making it about some woman. And Wilson convinced me, but I told them—"

"Loudly," Wilson teased.

"—that if they added some mushy love scene with the chick, I'd claw their eyes out." Steve grinned and everyone laughed.

"It's true. The director changed one of the scenes so that it's more a fade to black, with the bedroom door closing. It made the movie better, because if they'd have included the love scene, the rating would have been PG-13, and instead it was PG and more people went to see it." Wilson and Steve were obviously holding hands, and Quinn saw Marty watching them.

"Don't you worry about holding hands in public?" Marty asked, and Steve looked down at the table, like he'd just realized they were doing it.

"Everyone knows," Wilson explained. "My coming out was front-page news. For a while, a lot of people made a big deal out of it, but now everyone knows, so we don't pay it much mind. I spent a lot of years hiding who I was, and it made me miserable. I bought a place here to try to find a place where I could be happy, and I met Steve, which was the best thing that could possibly have happened."

The server approached the table, and they all picked up their menus. It was late, so they ordered appetizers and drinks, and the server left with a smile.

"But what about your family?" Marty asked. Quinn had hoped that seeing another happy gay couple who were comfortable with each other the way Wally and Dakota were would help Marty, and he was pleased to see that everyone seemed comfortable enough to talk. Quinn knew that Wilson had talked to schools and other groups around town regarding what it meant to be gay, so he'd expected this meeting would go well, but this was even better than he imagined.

"It's just me," Wilson said. "Now, Steve's father was another matter, but you can't live your life for someone else. If you do, you'll end up like I was: alone, miserable, and probably drinking a little too much to forget." The server returned with their beverages, placed them on the table, and then left once again. "I'd stopped writing music and was actually thinking I couldn't write anything anymore, and then I met Steve and the music began to play again. I wrote songs that have been made into movies because I let what was in my heart free rather than hiding from it." Steve patted Wilson's hand, and he smiled. "Okay, that's enough about me. What do you love to do?" Wilson asked Marty, and Quinn saw Marty's smile fade slightly.

"I used to play basketball. That was what I loved most in the world."

"What happened?" Steve asked softly. "You don't have to talk about it if you don't want to, but you look like a man with something to get off his chest."

"I had a stroke right there on the basketball court during my first college game. I worked all my life so I could play, and the first game I get to play, I have it all taken away." Quinn saw Marty's knuckles whiten as he clutched the arms of his chair.

"It's okay," Quinn said, and Marty turned toward him, his eyes blazing.

"Okay? It's not okay. It was a crappy thing to happen, and I wish it hadn't." Marty's scowl softened and he looked away. "Sorry, I spent hours with psychologists, and I thought I was over my anger issues. I guess there was still some hanging around."

"That was you?" Steve asked. "Your story made the news when you collapsed on the court. They said you'd had a stroke at eighteen and then there was nothing more said in the news." Steve looked at Wilson, who nodded slowly. "So Senator Green is your father."

"Yes."

"And you're working at Wally and Dakota's?" Wilson asked.

"Yes," Quinn answered. "He's been there for about two weeks." He looked to Marty for confirmation.

"Does your father know where you are?" Wilson asked.

"Yes. He and Dakota had met at one point or other, and when Dakota offered me the job, he said I had to get my father's blessing," Marty said.

"Does he know Wally and Dakota are gay?" Steve asked, and Quinn saw Marty shrug.

"I don't know what he knows. My dad knows a lot of people, and he has a staff that can check anyone out, so I guess I assumed that he knew, but I didn't know until I arrived and Wally rushed into Dakota's arms." Marty colored slightly but didn't look away. "So maybe he doesn't. I haven't brought it up with him and I really don't intend to. I like it here and I don't want to cause trouble for anyone."

Wilson and Steve shared a look that Quinn couldn't read, and then the server brought their appetizers, set them on the table, and passed a small plate to each of them. It seemed like a good time to change the subject.

"Are you going to make any more movies?" Quinn asked Wilson as he took a potato skin from the platter in the center of the table.

"Yes," Wilson answered with a glance at Steve. "*Walking Away From Me* was such a huge success that they want me to do three more." Wilson took a few chips off the plate and a small spoonful of artichoke dip, but didn't eat anything. "I enjoyed most of the process of making the movie, but Steve has to stay here to take care of the ranch and I'm either on location or in Hollywood, and being apart isn't particularly fun. I'll probably make the movies, because it means that once they're done, I can make my music and neither of us will have to worry about money for the rest of our lives. And that's the only reason I'm doing them."

"Doesn't Steve visit?" Marty asked.

"He does, but the visits are usually short. He has his horses to train and things to take care of here, so we end up being apart. *Walking Away From Me* took two months to film, and while I wasn't on the set for the entire movie, I was there for a lot, and it's sort of like the military—a lot of hurry up and wait. Then there was looping, where small bits of dialogue get fixed, and even callbacks for extra close-ups that they found they needed. That doesn't take into account the promotion, talk shows, and God knows what else I did." Steve patted Wilson's hand. "I know it sounds like I'm whining, but it isn't all as fun as most people would like to think. Making a movie is a ton of work for everyone, and most of it meant I was away from home."

"Do you have a house in Hollywood?" Marty asked, and Wilson shook his head.

"I keep an apartment in a secure building and maintain a low profile while I'm there." Wilson quieted and ate a few chips while the others scarfed down their food. "What I really love is the music."

"We built a studio onto the house, and the guys come in for rehearsals and recordings," Steve explained. "Those are the times when he's happiest."

"Hey, I'm always happy when you're around," Wilson corrected.

"I know, but you're even happier when Hammer, Freed, and Peter are around so you can make all the music you want. He has a concert tour planned for next year that will coincide with the release of the next movie. The whole thing is nuts."

Marty scoffed, and everyone looked at him. "That's nothing. There's nothing more nuts than Congress. Last year, Dad told me that they spent two days arguing over whether a bill should be worded for 'people sixty-five and over' or 'not for people less than sixty-five'. They actually argued over something that means the same thing. But they argued over it. How my dad can stand to do that year after year is beyond me. The entire system is designed so that nothing ever gets done unless it's a crisis, and then they're almost guaranteed to make the wrong decision or one that makes no one happy." Marty rolled his eyes dramatically. "Dad gets so angry sometimes because no one will compromise even when it's obviously in the best interest of the country."

"Isn't your dad up for reelection this year?" Quinn asked.

"Yup, and he's really nervous," Marty answered. "The primary is in May, and while he doesn't have a challenger yet, he's expecting one from the Tea Party, and they've been really nasty the last few cycles."

Quinn wondered just what Marty's Republican father would think of having a gay son, and how he'd treat him. As he sat next to Marty, he knew Marty had to be wondering just how his family would react to the truth about their son too. Quinn couldn't really remember Marty's dad being particularly vocal on the subject, but in an election year, your son coming out of the closet could open a kettle of worms and force a politician to take a position that would make no one happy, especially his son. Quinn glanced at Marty, biting his lower lip slightly. When he'd arranged for Steve and Wilson to meet them for appetizers, he hadn't expected the conversation to veer into deeper subjects.

"So how did you meet Dakota?" Wilson asked Marty.

"He and my doctor went to medical school together, and after I got out of the hospital, I didn't really want to go home. My mom tends to be a bit overprotective, and she would drive me crazy after all those months hovering over me while I was in the hospital." Marty finished the last of his food and set his plate aside. "In fact, I'm sort of surprised that she hasn't tried to arrange for a visit. I bet the only reason she hasn't is because Cassie and Josh are still in school. Although, who knows, she could call tomorrow and tell me she'll be in town this weekend." Marty seemed to realize just what that would mean, and Quinn heard him sigh. As soon as she showed up, the party—and some of Marty's newly acquired freedom—would be over unless he was willing to fight for it.

They finished their drinks and Quinn paid the check, over Wilson and Steve's objections. He'd invited them, after all, and it was the right thing to do. They all got their coats, and after saying good night, Marty and Quinn made their way back toward the car. Quinn helped Marty inside, and after placing his chair in the back, he got in and they headed back toward the ranch.

"That was amazing. I can't believe I got to meet Willie Meadows," Marty said, gushing slightly.

"You didn't—you got to meet Wilson. 'Willie Meadows' is a stage persona that really doesn't exist. The real person is the one you met tonight. That's pretty special, because not many people actually get to see that side of him. He's very protective of his privacy." Quinn turned the corner and drove down the dark road that led to Dakota and Wally's.

"You really did all this for me?" Marty asked.

"Of course. I wanted you to have a good time, and Steve has been trying to get together for a while. We were simply lucky they were free. Both of them are really busy people, but everything worked out," Quinn said, and he slowed the truck and made the turn into the ranch drive. Once he'd parked next to the other vehicles, Quinn helped Marty into his chair and then followed him up the ramp and inside. Wally and Dakota were still up, which was a bit of a surprise. They were usually "early to bed and early to rise" type people.

"Did you have a good time?" Dakota asked as he tried to disentangle himself from Wally, but the smaller man was having none of it.

"Yes, we did," Marty answered with a smile. Wally smiled back and then stood up as he and Dakota made their way toward the bedroom. "Night." Both Dakota and Wally smiled as they vacated the room, leaving the two of them alone. "Sometimes I think Wally and my mother are related."

"He definitely has mother-hen tendencies," Quinn said as he settled on the sofa next to Marty's chair. "So, you won the preview game. What kind of prize do you want?" Quinn leaned over the arm, and Marty smiled at him.

"What are my choices?" Marty asked, and Quinn leaned closer, lightly touching his lips to Marty's. The kiss was soft and rather fleeting, but Quinn didn't want to spook Marty.

"That's one of them," Quinn said, and Marty moved closer once again, making his choice clear through his actions. Marty's lips were warm and moist as they kissed again, this time a little harder. Quinn could taste a bit of the food they'd eaten before, but mostly what he got was full-on Marty. He tasted sweet and slightly spicy, with just a touch of heat simmering right beneath the surface. When they parted, Marty smiled at him, and Quinn settled on the sofa cushion, taking Marty's hand as they watched the last of the program.

The news came on afterward, leading off with stories of local interest before turning to the national news. "Senator William Green gave an impassioned speech on the floor of the Senate today in support of traditional family values." The picture changed, and Quinn saw Marty's father standing on the floor of the Senate.

"Our values and those of our children are being corrupted and twisted to the point that none of us will recognize them in just a few short years, and that is why I am championing the cause of a constitutional amendment to clarify once and for all that marriage in this country should and will consist of the union of one man to one woman," Marty's father said with all the passion of a southern preacher. The camera returned to the announcer, who prattled on for a few seconds before moving on to the next story.

Quinn was a bit stunned, and he cautioned a glance at Marty, who looked almost stricken. The color had drained from his face. "It's okay, Marty, often that stuff is just talk."

Marty looked at him, and Quinn moved away as Marty shook his head, "My dad is never just talk. He's one of the most powerful men in the Senate, and what he says carries weight." Marty released the brakes from his chair. "I had no idea he actually felt that way." Marty slowly backed away from the sofa. "I think I should say good night now."

Quinn nodded and stood up, then walked toward the door. "I'll see you tomorrow."

"Okay," Marty said with a hard swallow, and then he disappeared down the hallway. Quinn left the house and walked to his truck, tempted to pound the side of it as he thought of Marty's father ruining their amazing evening. And to top it off, Quinn knew that this bit of news was going to make Marty even more tentative, if it didn't outright shut the door on his initial explorations once and for all.

Chapter Four

MARTY had spent the past two days avoiding everyone he possibly could, especially Quinn. Their date had been wonderful, and he'd had a great time at the movies, and meeting Willie Meadows. And the kiss—his first real kiss. Then he'd heard all that crap his own father was spouting, and unfortunately it hadn't stopped with that one newscast. Every single channel on the television and radio touted his father's newly articulated stance on, well, people like Marty and the people who'd been so nice to him. He'd thought numerous times that he should just call his family and arrange to go home. At least then, he could more easily pretend he wasn't who he was and he could somehow be who his family expected him to be. After getting out of bed, he got himself into his chair and managed to work his robe around himself before making his way quietly into Jefferson's room and its handicap-equipped bathroom.

Marty cleaned up before taking a shower. He'd hoped the warm water would relax away some of the anxiety that had been building and building, but it did nothing at all. After turning off the water, he got out and dried off, and then put on his robe once again before hanging up his towels and getting ready to leave. On his way out, he did what he'd been trying to avoid since he'd come into the room—he looked at himself in the mirror. Marty had half expected that he'd somehow look different. That the warm feeling he got when he thought about Quinn and the way he'd treated him and kissed him would somehow show on his face, but of course it didn't. Still, Marty had a difficult time looking himself in the eye. Turning away quickly, he opened the bathroom door and quietly made his way past Jefferson's hospital bed on his way back to his room.

"Marty," Jefferson called to him softly, and he wheeled himself to where Jefferson could see him. "There's something wrong," he stated in a sleep-rasped voice. "I know there is, and you can't tell me different. For two weeks, you were happy, and now you barely look at anyone." Marty lifted his gaze from his feet. "Don't bother denying it. I've seen that same look on most of you boys at one time or other, and I watch the news, so I can guess what's got you bothered."

"My dad hates me," Marty said softly. "He's opened some crusade against me and people like me." Marty heard Jefferson take a slow deep breath.

"Your daddy doesn't hate you, not one bit. From what you've said, your momma and daddy love you very much, and I don't doubt that for a minute. You shouldn't think that because you like colts instead of fillies you shouldn't get to love, or be loved, either. Bein' gay here ain't easy. Dakota and Wally have stood up and fought for themselves more than once, and in more ways than I want to imagine."

"But what do I do about my dad?"

"Nothing," Jefferson answered, and Marty felt a bent, calloused hand take his very lightly. "There's nothing you can do about your dad, and no one here expects you to do anything. But… and I told this same thing to Dakota once… you need to be who you are regardless of your daddy, momma, or all the lard-heads in Washington. You can only live a good life if you live it freely and honestly."

"So I should tell my father," Marty said, a jolt of fear running through him.

"Eventually, yes. But to start with, you need to allow yourself to accept and celebrate the person you are. And there ain't no place better to do that than right where you are, right now. There's safety in numbers, and when you're ready and feel good about yourself, you can have the conversation with your daddy that the thought of having right now is making your gut churn."

Marty nodded slowly. Jefferson was probably right. But he'd never kept secrets from his dad. Even when he'd done something wrong, he'd confessed and owned up to it rather than keeping secrets or hiding. And now that he understood things better, he wanted to talk to his father. "But isn't that lying?"

"No. It's finding out who you are. And you need to know that before you can do anything else. Once you do, you can let your family get to know the real you, in your own time." Jefferson gasped slightly and quieted. Marty wondered if he was okay, but he rolled his head slightly on the pillow and smiled his crooked smile at Marty.

"Sometimes I wish you were my dad," Marty said softly, choking up at the support he was receiving from a man he'd only known a few weeks.

"We don't get to pick our family, so thank God we get to choose our friends," Jefferson said, shaking Marty's hand slightly. Jefferson closed his eyes, releasing Marty's hand. Marty left the room quietly and went to the one he was using, got dressed, and then wheeled himself into the kitchen for a cup of coffee before carefully making his way to the barn on a bright, sunny spring morning.

He did all his chores, making sure the horses had food, water, and a treat. By the time he was done, Dakota was ready to go into the office, and he gave Marty a ride to town.

Therapy was a painful, arduous process that pushed aside all thoughts of anything except somehow getting to the other side of those parallel bars in one piece.

"Your arms aren't as strong as I'd like," Johnny, his therapist, told him once they were done on the bars. "I could see them shaking a number of times, and you could hurt yourself. We need to work on those, and next time, we'll use some of the machines to help rebuild your lost motor pathways."

"I want to walk again," Marty said after collapsing back into his wheelchair once he'd made it to the end. He'd actually taken a few tentative steps, but mostly it had been Johnny simply moving his legs.

"I know you do, but you need to take it at a pace your body can handle." Johnny handed him a small dumbbell. "I want you to curl this ten times in each arm, and then do ten triceps extensions with each arm." Johnny demonstrated each exercise for him. "Don't worry. We're going to get you walking again, but it's going to take time." Marty sighed, but did the exercises the way Johnny had showed him. "After a rest, see if you can do it again." Johnny seemed to have the patience of a saint. "Hurting yourself because you're going too fast is not going to help you walk again."

"I know," Marty grumbled as he picked up the weights again and went through the movements for the second time.

"What's got you in an all-fired hurry, anyway? You're usually intense, but patient and careful. Today you can't sit still and are suddenly in a real rush." Johnny watched him do the exercise, correcting him slightly as he tired.

"Just nerved up, I guess," Marty answered, finishing the set more carefully.

"Rest a little and do the last set, then we're done for the day," Johnny said as he stood up and walked over to his desk.

"Remember to do the exercise slowly and get the most out of each rep." Johnny picked up a clipboard and began writing while Marty did the last set as slowly as he could. It was almost embarrassing how little weight he could lift at the moment. He used to curl thirty and forty pounds, but now ten and fifteen were a struggle. When he was done, he put down the weight.

"I know it seems light, but your body has been through a lot," Johnny said. "Give yourself time. It could take months or years for you to get back most of what you lost, you know that."

Marty nodded, but didn't answer. "I feel trapped sometimes."

"Is it the chair? Because that's just transportation, not part of who you are." Johnny tossed the clipboard onto the desk with a clatter.

"The chair, my family, even Quinn a little," Marty admitted.

"I can understand about the chair and even your family. Because I swear, families were put on this earth to drive us all crazy. Lord knows mine was. But what has Quinn done to make you feel trapped?" Johnny leaned his butt against the desk.

Marty shrugged. It was hard to put into words. But Johnny simply looked at him and obviously wasn't going to let it go. He'd learned almost immediately that Johnny was part physical therapist and part shoulder to cry on. "I don't know," Marty answered.

"I think you do. Could it be that Quinn is what brings the way you feel about your family into focus?"

Reluctantly, Marty nodded. "They're so different, and I feel like if I choose to be the person I want to be around Quinn, then I can't be what my family expects."

"Puh-lease…." In that moment, Johnny sounded so gay it made Marty laugh. "It's what *you* expect of you that matters. Your family is your family, but you can't live your life for them."

"That's what Dakota's dad told me," Marty said, and Johnny smiled and nodded.

"Wisest man I know. Half the people who've met him wish he was their father, me included." Johnny straightened back up. "If you want my two cents, give Quinn and yourself a break. You can't solve the problems of the world, or even your family. Just concentrate on yourself and what you feel is important, and everything will be fine."

Marty knew Johnny was right, but that was easier said than done. His family was important to him, and he didn't want to let them down. He knew coming out as gay would do just that, as well as embarrass his father politically. Granted, it wasn't the same as if his father had come out as gay or something, but it would raise questions around his family that his dad didn't need in an election year. "I'll try."

"That's all anyone can do," Johnny told him as Marty got ready to leave. "How are you getting back?"

"Dakota said someone would be here to pick me up," Marty answered and wheeled himself through the office and out front, where he saw Quinn's truck waiting for him. Immediately he knew he'd most likely been set up. Still, he needed to talk with Quinn. The past two days had been hard, because although he'd wanted to see Quinn and spend time with him, Marty had been so conflicted. He still was, but he'd decided to take Johnny's advice, and he was only going to learn about himself if he figured out what made him happy. And being with Quinn had definitely done that.

Marty wheeled himself toward the truck. As he got closer, he saw Quinn's stern expression and he couldn't help snickering slightly. Quinn looked so dour that Marty couldn't help thinking it was some sort of affectation.

"What's so funny?" Quinn asked accusingly, his scowl softening.

"Nothing. You look sort of cute when you're angry." That seemed to break the tension, and Quinn rolled his eyes.

"I wouldn't be angry if you hadn't refused to look at me for two days." Quinn opened the passenger door and then approached where Marty was waiting. After lifting him out of the chair, Quinn carefully set Marty on the seat before putting the chair in the back. Marty pulled the door closed and waited for Quinn to join him. He wasn't sure how well he could explain things to Quinn, but he knew he had to try.

The driver's door opened and Quinn climbed in, then slammed the door behind him.

"I'm sorry. I should have tried to explain." Quinn didn't start the engine, but he wouldn't look at him, either. "It's just really complicated. I was brought up with my dad in public office. My mom and dad drilled into my head that you always do your best, earn what you get on your own merit, avoid the appearance of impropriety, and never do anything that could embarrass the family or cause questions that can't be easily answered and verified. When I saw my dad make that speech, all I could think of was that no matter what I did, I was going to cause my family more pain and trouble than you can imagine." His stomach clenched and he slowly began breathing through his mouth.

"Is that all you have to say?" Quinn asked and then started the engine. "I'll take you back to the ranch."

"I don't know what else to tell you. I shouldn't have ignored you for the past two days, but I ignored everyone. I thought I could go back into my shell and everything would be the same as it had been before I got here, but it can't. Eventually my family will find out about me, and who knows how they'll react." Marty stared out the side window, his stomach continuing to churn as Quinn turned onto the main road.

"Do you think your family will disown you because of this?" Quinn asked.

"I hope not," Marty answered honestly. "I would hope I'm more important to my parents than that, but I really don't know. I honestly don't know." The trapped feelings he'd had for the last two days surrounded him, pressing on all sides. "Stop the truck!" Quinn pulled off, and Marty opened the door, holding it as he leaned out and emptied the contents of his stomach alongside the truck. Somehow he managed not to fall out, and then he felt Quinn holding him, steadying him as he gasped for breath.

"Here," Quinn said, handing him a tissue. "It's okay."

"No, it's not," Marty gasped. "I've spent the past two days trying to figure out a way it can be okay, and the only one I can think of is to go home. But that would be running away, and I know the problem will just follow me regardless, I know that." He wiped his mouth and sat back, closing the door. Quinn sat next to him, holding Marty tightly.

"Everyone keeps telling me that I need to figure out who I am, but I already know who I am. I'm Martin Green, the son of Senator William Green, and that's who I have to be. I can't be anyone else." Marty willed himself not to cry, and for the most part, he succeeded.

"You are more than just your father's son. You're you, and you need to take some time to figure out who that is. Why do you think Dakota offered you the job? He doesn't need help on the ranch; he has lots of it, and people ask to work here all the time. Dakota and Wally are the biggest-hearted people I have ever met. I know you haven't seen them yet, but Wally rescues lions and tigers from circuses or people who thought they'd make good pets because he feels they should have good lives. The two of them have helped everyone on the ranch in one way or another, including me."

"What did they do for you?"

"Gave me a job I love and a place where I can get away from my father. When I started working for Wally, I didn't have much experience or education. He worked with me and helped me take classes so I could become his assistant. They have this way of seeing what people can become and helping them. I suspect Dakota saw some of that in you too." Quinn continued holding him, and Marty leaned into the touch. "You aren't alone. You have a lot of people here who like you and are willing to help, because at some point, we've all been where you are."

"That's sort of what Jefferson said this morning."

"Then stop worrying about everything and enjoy yourself and the time you have. Your family can't live your life for you any more than I can live my life taking care of my adolescent-acting father." Marty wondered what Quinn meant, but he felt too good in Quinn's embrace to question it. Closing his eyes, he just enjoyed sitting there as they listened to the truck engine run.

"I'll try," Marty finally said, and he realized he'd been saying that a lot today. Maybe it was time he really did it. Maybe everyone was right and he needed to experience things on his own without worrying about what his family would think. It wasn't like everyone at the ranch would alert the news media or anything. Marty rested his head on Quinn's shoulder and continued to hold him for a while. "This is really nice."

"It is, but I need to get you back to the ranch, and I need to help Wally with some appointments, but maybe we can pick this up after dinner."

"Okay," Marty agreed, swallowing hard. "I need to check on the horses, and I promised to finish the Louis L'Amour book I'd started reading to Jefferson." Quinn released him, and Marty wished he were still being held. He felt safe in Quinn's arms. But at least he was calmer now, and he could think. He still couldn't reconcile the feelings he was having for Quinn and what he knew about himself with what his family expected, but their expectations were theirs.

Quinn slid back behind the wheel and placed the truck into gear, and they started to move again. "You have friends, Marty," Quinn said as he reached over and interlaced their fingers, and Marty nodded slowly. Quinn drove one-handed most of the way back to the ranch, and Marty tightened his grip, watching where their hands touched the entire time.

When they arrived, Quinn helped him out of the truck and into his chair before bending down to give him a hug. "I'll see you later, and if you want to talk some more, I'll listen."

"Thank you," Marty said, but he wasn't too sure how much he still had to talk about. "I think I'm going to be all right now." Marty took a deep breath and hugged Quinn one more time before he wheeled himself into the house, with Quinn walking behind him. Once inside, Marty went right to his room and took off his coat before wheeling himself into Jefferson's room, where he found him asleep. Marty was about to turn his chair around and leave when he saw Jefferson's eyes slide open. "Do you need anything?"

Jefferson rolled his head on the pillow, and Marty could tell he was tired, but knew exactly when his eyes shifted to the book resting on the nightstand. Marty picked it up and positioned his chair near the light, and then started to read. The pace of the story and the quiet of the room lulled away most of his nerves and residual fear. His thoughts settled as the story wound around him. By the time he'd finished the book, the bad guys had been vanquished, the hero had gotten the girl, and all was right in the world. Jefferson's eyes were closed, but somehow Marty knew he was awake.

"You're a good boy, Marty," Jefferson said.

"Thank you," Marty said, and Jefferson extended his curled hand. Marty reached out and held it lightly in his. "Quinn and

Johnny told me the same thing you did, and I'm trying to take your advice."

"Opinions are like assholes—everyone has one and everyone thinks theirs don't stink. You listen to your heart and not me, or anyone else." Jefferson's voice trailed off, and Marty chuckled softly. "I'm going to go back to sleep until the nurse comes to poke and prod me again." Jefferson turned away, and Marty placed the book in the pocket on his wheelchair. Reminding himself to get another one from the bookshelves in the living room, he quietly left the room and wheeled himself through the silent house.

As he'd first noticed when he'd arrived, the house was nothing like the one he'd grown up in, but neither were the people. There was no division between the public and private persona with any of these people—they were as you found them, and as genuine and honest as they came. None of them had an ulterior motive for anything. The house and furniture were as comfortable and real as everyone who lived here, unlike the huge house he'd grown up in, where there were rooms he'd never been allowed to go in as a child because they were for show. Marty wheeled himself up to the homemade bookshelf and replaced the book he'd read, then placed another in the bag so he could read it to Jefferson when he was ready. What amazed Marty most was how comfortable he felt here, like he belonged.

"Marty." Dakota came in, the door banging behind him. "Is Dad asleep?"

"Yes," Marty answered and turned his chair to face Dakota. "Is he doing okay? Your dad seems to sleep most of the time, and when I'm reading to him, he can only pay attention for short periods of time." Marty hoped his concern came through in his voice and that Dakota didn't think he was butting into private business.

Dakota sat on the end of the sofa closest to him. "Dad has had MS for quite a while now, and his body is starting to shut down. He lost his legs years ago, and after that, he improved for a while. We were also able to get some improvements through medication, but we've exhausted our options, so now it's a matter of making sure he's as comfortable as possible and able to do whatever he can. I don't know how much longer he has, but I'm convinced that he isn't going to improve again. So we're making the most of the time he has. And that's part of the reason you're here. I don't want him spending his days alone with a nurse. I've seen you with him, and you talk to him and listen to him. Even the times when he can be hard to understand, you still listen." Dakota looked toward the hallway and sighed. "He's my dad, and I love him so very much. He accepted me… and Wally… with almost no questions asked."

"If I can ask, why don't you spend more time with him?" Marty inquired, half expecting to get yelled at, but Dakota simply shook his head.

"I spend a lot of time with him, but I can't be here during the day because I have patients to see." Dakota sighed softly. "When Dad first got sick, I dropped out of medical school to return, run the ranch, and help take care of him. And I did it without a second thought—he's my dad. After a few years, there were other people to care for him, and he insisted I return to school. He wanted me to finish medical school and become a doctor more than anything. It had been my dream for a long time, and he wanted that to come true." Dakota shifted in this chair. "You see, he hid his disease from me for as long as he could so I would continue school. When I was able to return with Wally's support and help, Dad insisted I go, and even now, he insists that I go in to work and build up the practice. I haven't told him that I've been turning away patients so the practice wouldn't get too large and I can spend more time here with him. He'd be so pissed at me if he knew."

"I don't get it. He seems to love the time you spend with him," Marty commented, thinking of the time he and his dad had spent together when he was younger. It had been a while since they'd explored parts of the backwoods of Yellowstone, or camped in the Grand Tetons, like they had when Marty was younger.

"I didn't at first, either, but he doesn't want to be a burden on anyone, and more than anything, he's as proud as he can be that I became a doctor and have a good life. He knows that he could very easily become the focus of everything around here. That his care could become what everything else revolves around, and he'd kill me if I let that happen. Dad's a proud man, and he knows that he only has a limited time left, but he wants to live it with as much dignity and independence as he can. You give him that, because the two of you have a relationship that's independent of me and everyone else here." Dakota swallowed hard.

"How much longer do you think he has?" Marty asked carefully, closing his eyes at the thought.

"It's hard to say. His systems have found it harder and harder to simply keep up with his body's needs for a while now," Dakota explained, his voice becoming ragged. "Maybe a year, if we're lucky. I know this sounds harsh, but I hope when he goes, he has a heart attack or a massive stroke and dies in his sleep without lingering on and on. He could hang on for years, dying by inches, and I don't want that for him." Dakota stood up, and Marty watched him leave the room and head down the hallway, and Marty knew he was going to visit his dad. Marty knew if Dakota hadn't, then he would have, because he felt the need to return to Jefferson's room and simply sit with him for a while, even if he was sleeping. He'd been on the ranch only a matter of weeks, but Marty knew there would be a hole in his heart when that time came.

Marty was about to put on his coat when he heard Dakota coming back down the hall.

"I'm heading back into the office. Dad will be asleep for a while."

"Then I'll go out and see if I can help in the barn for a while. When he wakes up, I have another book for us to read," Marty explained, and Dakota squeezed his shoulder lightly before shrugging on the coat he'd left over the back of one of the chairs and leaving the house, closing the door quietly behind him. Marty got his own coat and gloves, putting them on before following behind. He made his way across the yard and into the barn. He needed something to take his mind off everything. Activity and work had always helped in the past, and today was no exception. Sure, it took him longer to do things than the other guys, but the guys didn't mind, and Marty knew they appreciated the help. He was just finishing up when his phone rang, the display showing it was his father.

"Hi, Dad," Marty answered, feeling a touch of the butterflies and dread he'd been feeling for the past two days return.

"How is everything? Are you getting on?" His dad asked the questions in rapid succession, with almost manic energy in his voice.

"Good. The therapist is strengthening my arms, and we're starting to work on walking. The ranch is great. I work in the barn helping to care for the horses, and I help take care of Dr. Holden's dad. He's really something—you'd like him a lot, I think." Marty didn't want his dad asking too many questions about the ranch. He wasn't sure how much his dad knew about Wally, Dakota, and the rest of their friends and extended family. "How's the campaign?"

"Rough. As I expected, I have a primary challenger who's playing the Washington outsider card and all fired up about changing things in government. I don't think he's really going to get much traction. We'll see how it goes. I've been through this before."

"I know, and you've done a lot of good," Marty said.

"Have you talked to your mother lately?" his dad asked, changing the subject quickly. Marty heard voices in the background and figured it was his dad's staff.

"Yes," Marty answered.

"Then you know she's itching to come pay you a visit," his dad said, and Marty groaned inwardly.

"I know. But I'm fine, I really am," he said quickly as his stomach jumped. "I'm doing well, the therapy's good, and I like it here."

"Your mother worries," his dad said.

"I know, but I'm an adult and I need to be able to take care of myself for a while. I'm learning to do things I've never had to do before, and I like it," Marty said, trying not to let how much he didn't want his mother to visit to show in his voice. If he was too vehement, his father would wonder why.

"I'll put her off for a while," he said. "But you call if you need anything."

"I will," Marty agreed, and he heard a shuffle.

"Hi, Marty," Cassie said into the phone. "I miss you. Can you walk yet?"

Marty smiled. "Not yet, but I'm learning."

"Do they have horses there?" Cassie asked excitedly.

"Yes. They have cattle too, and there's also lions and tigers," Marty explained.

"Real ones?" Cassie asked with a touch of awe and disbelief.

"Yes, real ones. They save them from circuses and give them a good home. I haven't seen them up close yet, but sometimes I can hear it when the lion roars." Marty heard Cassie squeal and ask if she could pet them if she came to visit, and Marty explained that they weren't pet lion and tigers, but if she came to visit, she could see them if she wanted. He heard the phone shuffle again, and then his father came back on the line.

"I have to go, but you take care and we'll talk soon," his father said, and Marty said good-bye before ending the call. Marty put the phone away, pushing away the worry, which got easier when Quinn strode through the barn carrying one of the cases of veterinary supplies.

"You look like you're feeling better," Quinn said as he approached, and Marty angled his head upward, hoping Quinn would take the hint. He did, kissing him lightly on the lips.

"I am," Marty answered with a smile once Quinn pulled away. "I've had some time to think, and I'm sorry about the past few days. I shouldn't have pushed you and everyone else away."

Quinn kissed him again. "You're forgiven, but don't do it again, okay?" Quinn smiled when he straightened up. "I have to put all this away. Do you have things to do yet?"

"I need to read to Jefferson this afternoon, but unless anyone has something they need, I'm pretty free."

"Good," Quinn said with a hint of mischief in his expression. "I'll see you later." Quinn hurried toward Wally's clinic at the back of the barn, and Marty watched him go before returning to the house. Jefferson was awake, and Marty spent much of the rest of the afternoon in Jefferson's room, reading and spending time. The nurse stopped in before dinner, and Marty left her to take care of what Jefferson needed and wheeled himself into the kitchen to help Wally with dinner.

"Are you staying?' Wally asked Quinn as they were starting to set the table.

"If it's okay," Quinn answered, and Wally handed Marty another place setting.

"You're always welcome; you know that," Wally said, and Marty moved the places around slightly on the table to make room for one more. Once everything was ready, they sat down for a talkative dinner, with everyone telling about their day and plans for the next week. His family meals had always been quiet and rather sedate, but Marty loved the discussion and the way people asked for and listened to his opinion here. When the meal was over, Wally shooed everyone out of the kitchen, so Marty went into the living room and Quinn helped him get out of his chair so he could sit on the sofa. It felt nice to sit on regular furniture again, and even better when Quinn sat next to him.

Marty leaned against Quinn, who held him gently. "This is nice," Quinn observed, and Marty hummed his agreement as others joined them.

"How are things with your dad?" Marty asked, and Quinn groaned softly. "Okay, sorry I asked."

"The same," Quinn said. "I tried to broach the subject with him about me moving here, but he didn't want to hear it and proceeded to get ready to go out for the evening. At least I told him, and whether he wants it or not, I'm moving out. The only thing that worries me are the animals."

"Then bring yours with you," Wally said. "We have room for a few horses and whatever other critters are yours."

"Thanks, but I'm worried about my dad's too. He'll end up neglecting them if I'm not there." Quinn sounded genuinely concerned, and Marty looked at Wally, hoping he had another answer.

"Don't you worry about that. If you move in here, I'll pay your father a little visit. If he even thinks of neglecting his animals, I'll have every one of them removed from his place so fast it'll make his head spin." Wally sat next to Dakota, and Marty noticed that once again they were as close to each other as two people could be and still have their clothes on. Marty noticed that Quinn moved a little closer too, and they watched television for a while, just the four of them. Marty quickly found that he loved being held like this. Quinn's scent surrounded him, and every time he inhaled, he caught Quinn's richness on the air. Before coming to the ranch, Marty hadn't known that a relationship like Wally and Dakota's was even possible, and now as he peeked at them occasionally, he knew it was what he wanted.

Wally settled almost in Dakota's lap, with the bigger man's arms around him, and they both yawned at the same time. Without saying anything to each other, both Wally and Dakota got up and said their good-nights before disappearing down the hallway, the sound of their bedroom door closing following shortly behind.

Marty turned his attention to Quinn, who seemed to be looking at him expectantly. Marty yawned, and Quinn held him tighter. He knew what Quinn was asking, and Marty was about two seconds from saying yes when Quinn's phone rang.

Quinn didn't shift as he pulled out his phone. "Hello, Dad," Quinn said into the phone, and Marty heard Quinn's father's muffled voice. He was speaking loudly, and while Marty couldn't make out the words, he could hear the almost panicked tone in his voice. "Dad, calm down and tell me what happened from the beginning." Marty felt Quinn stiffen next to him, tension building throughout his body. "Was it a wolf?" Quinn listened a little while longer. "Okay, I'll be there as soon as I can." Quinn ended the call and shoved his phone back into his pants. "I need to see what's going on. Dad says he saw a wolf and that the animals are riled up and stomping." Marty leaned close, kissing him lightly. "I'll see you later."

Marty swallowed and nodded, noting the definite disappointment in Quinn's eyes. He felt the same way, and when Quinn pulled away, Marty tugged him back into a kiss that was anything but soft and gentle. He mashed his lips to Quinn's, holding him around the neck as he took what he wanted from the kiss. They were both breathing hard, and Marty saw Quinn's wide pupils and watched him swallow hard as he moved away. Quinn stood up, and Marty watched as he shrugged on his coat and then hurried out the front door. He'd finally gotten up the courage and pushed his worries far enough back that he could act on the desire simmering inside of him, and now Quinn had to leave. The timing was just freaking perfect.

Chapter Five

QUINN usually hated leaving Wally and Dakota's place to head home, but tonight he wanted to scream. Not only because his father had interrupted them, but walking with a hard-on because of that kiss from Marty was almost enough to make him turn around and wait until the morning to look into what was happening. But he couldn't do that. The animals might be in danger, and Lord knew what his father was doing to stir them up further. He got into his truck, slammed the door, and took off, driving as fast as he dared toward home.

When he pulled into the driveway, he saw his father standing between the house and the small barn, carrying a gun and looking around like he was on some sort of guard duty. Quinn pulled to a stop and got out. "What's going on?"

"I came out to check on the horses and I scared up a wolf. He ran off that way, and I've been out here waiting for you in case he shows up again."

Quinn looked in the direction his father indicated, then walked through the melting snow. He didn't see wolf tracks heading away. But Quinn did see the tracks of one of the dogs that had run around the house, probably chasing the rabbit whose tracks he found on the same path. He wondered what his father had actually seen and what he was up to. His dad obviously knew the difference between one of their dogs and a wolf. As he walked back toward the barn, he reminded himself to check further for tracks when it was light. Ignoring his father, Quinn pulled open the barn door and looked inside.

The horses were calm, quietly extending their heads out of the stalls to see what Quinn was doing. They nuzzled him, wanting attention, but didn't seem upset or agitated. A wolf near the barn would certainly have had all of them skittish and probably stomping in their stalls. So either they'd calmed right down once the wolf had run off, or something else was going on. Quinn checked the mangers and water troughs, making sure they all had plenty to eat and drink before he turned out the lights and closed the barn door behind him. "Everything's fine," he told his father. "You better put the gun away before you manage to shoot your own foot."

"Don't be talking to me that way, boy," his father snapped, and Quinn ignored him as he walked toward the house.

"Why not? You're the one who acts like a teenager, boy," Quinn challenged, whirling around toward his father. Right then and there, Quinn made his decision. "I'm going to be moving out in the next week. Wally and Dakota are going to board my horses as part of my pay, so you'll only need to take care of yours."

His father glanced toward the barn and then back at him. "All the horses in that barn are mine," Quinn's father said. "I pay for their upkeep, so they're mine."

"Prove it," Quinn told him. "I have the papers, and if you try anything, we'll have the sheriff out here so fast your head will spin."

His father deflated like a balloon with a hole in it. "You can't leave."

"Of course I can, and I'm telling you I'll be moving out in a week—sooner if I can get my things together," Quinn said as the wind began to pick up, the cold cutting through his coat and jeans. Without arguing further, Quinn took the gun from his father's hands and then walked inside the house and placed the .22 in the gun case. He heard his father follow behind. He was too tired to argue this further, and angry that his father had called him home for nothing, so he went into the kitchen for something to drink and stopped in his tracks.

Every dish in the place appeared to be piled in the sink, waiting to be washed. There were pans on the stove with the remnants sticking to the bottoms from whatever his father had tried to cook and most likely burned. The trash was overflowing with bottles and other garbage.

"Jesus," Quinn groaned softly. He'd only been sleeping at home for the past week or so, going to work early and coming home late. He tried to remember the last time he'd been in the kitchen and realized it had been at least five days. "Can't you clean up anything?" Quinn asked as he stared.

"You do all that," his father said from the living room. Quinn heard the chair creak as his father plopped himself down, then the sound of the television switching on a few moments later.

"You're going to need to do all that yourself or you'll be up to your neck in your own dirt, because I'm not doing this anymore." Quinn left the kitchen and walked down the hall to his room, where he closed the door behind him and then flopped down on his bed. How on earth could he have missed how completely helpless and dependent his father had become? The man couldn't, or wouldn't, even do his own dishes. It had to be sheer laziness. When he'd lost his mother, Quinn had stepped up to take care of things around the house, and now his father was as dependent on him as he'd been on his mother.

Quinn fished his phone out of his pants and was about to call the ranch, but then remembered that Wally and Dakota were already in bed, and there was no need to wake up the entire ranch because he'd been having trouble with his father.

"Quinn, you going to make dinner?" His father's voice drifted through the door.

He got up off his bed and yanked open the door. "No. I already ate." He closed the door once again, and then, with a huff, got up and went back into the kitchen. He pulled open the refrigerator door and managed to find lunch meat and bread. Quinn slapped together two sandwiches and took them into the living room on the only clean plate he could find.

"Are you going to clean up before you go to bed?" his father asked as he lifted one of the sandwiches off the plate and took a bite before reaching for a beer. He'd go to the kitchen to get beer, but not to make something to eat. Quinn was about to tell his father what he could do with the dishes, but it wouldn't do anything except make him angry and he wasn't in the mood for a fight right now. So while Quinn did the fucking dishes and put everything away, making as much noise as possible, he planned how to best get everything that was important to him out of the house.

By the time he'd finished with everything and turned out the kitchen light, it was approaching midnight. More than anything, Quinn wanted to get in his truck and drive back to the ranch to see if Marty was still awake, but that seemed desperate, tacky, and like he was only interested in Marty for sex. And while the man was cute and really sexy, he also meant more to Quinn than just someone to take to bed. He'd see Marty tomorrow. Quinn went to his room, turning out the lights on the way and making sure everything was closed up. His father was already in bed, no light coming from under his door, when Quinn shuffled into his own room. After a quick cleanup, he undressed and climbed into bed, falling asleep almost immediately, remembering Marty's kiss and dreaming that Marty was sleeping next to him.

THE following morning, Quinn was up early. He packed what he could and loaded it into the back of his truck. He also took a look around the house and barn, but saw no sign of wolf tracks. The old fart couldn't tell the difference between a wolf and one of their own dogs. After feeding the horses, Quinn made sure all the animals had food and water, and gave the dogs a few scratches and pats, their tails whapping against his legs. "Aww, hell," Quinn said as he opened his door, holding it open. "Maxine, Dolly," he called, and the two mutts jumped into the truck. He wasn't going to leave them to the mercy of his father. He'd found them both as puppies and raised them himself. He was going to take his girls with him. After he climbed into the truck, he smiled as both of them put their front paws on the dashboard so they could see out, tongues lolling happily as Quinn put the truck in gear and carefully pulled down the driveway.

The girls weren't particularly used to riding, and once he got going, they prowled around the interior. "Sit down, both of you," Quinn said, and they sat on the seat for about two seconds before starting their prowling again. Finally, just as they approached the ranch, Maxine settled, looking out the window, while Dolly lay down on the seat.

"I take it you're staying," Wally commented with a grin as he approached the truck once Quinn had pulled to a stop and opened the door. Both dogs bounded out and immediately began sniffing around. Wally and Dakota's pack raced out. Maxine growled, and then Dolly raced away with all the other dogs on her heels, the whole lot of them playing like old doggie friends. Maxine stayed close to Quinn. "Did something happen?" Wally asked as he helped Quinn carry some of his things to the bunkhouse and into one of the empty rooms. Quinn had helped Dakota and Wally build it just last year for the few men who didn't live in town, and right now, two of the three bedrooms were empty.

"I think Dad's becoming even more dependent. I've been here for the past few days, and he didn't even do the dishes. I made him dinner at ten thirty last night because he didn't have the ambition to do it himself. I need to get away and be on my own. I hope it's okay that I brought Maxine and Dolly." He absently patted Maxine on the head, and she sat down next to him, her tail thumping lightly on the wood floor.

"Of course it is," Wally said, kneeling down.

"Careful, she's a...," Quinn began as Maxine ran her tongue up Wally's face, "...licker."

Wally simply laughed and stroked behind Maxine's ears before standing up again. "Let's get the rest of your things. Do you need help getting the horses? I can call Haven and see if he has time today to bring them over."

"If he isn't too busy," Quinn said. Haven and Dakota had merged their two ranches years ago, and Haven was the foreman for the entire operation. He and his partner, Phillip, were good friends of Quinn's. They'd also been busy getting ready for spring and making sure the cattle made it through the winter in good shape. "I haven't seen either Haven or Phillip in weeks."

"Phillip hibernates for most of the winter, and you know Haven, he worries and frets about the cattle during the cold, and now that the snow has really started melting, he's making sure that the cattle aren't in danger from any high water." Wally worked with Quinn to carry another load from the truck. "I have a call I need to make. It should be easy, so if you could check on the supplies in the truck, I'll make the call and you can finish unpacking or get another load if you need. I'll call Haven as I'm driving. You'll also need to pick up Marty from therapy."

"Is he going every day now?" Quinn asked as they walked toward the barn from the bunkhouse.

"Occupational therapy. They're trying to help him with his dexterity," Wally explained, and Quinn nodded before hurrying into the clinic to pack Wally's cases and get them in the truck.

Once he was done, they loaded them, and then Wally drove off. Quinn finished up in the clinic, doing a quick inventory for Wally so he could place a supply order before getting back into his truck and heading back to his father's place. Inside, he packed the rest of the things he was taking with him and then drove to Dakota's office, where he saw Marty wheeling himself out of the door.

Quinn could not keep the smile from his face as Marty glided toward him. He leaned back against the truck, legs crossed slightly as he watched every move of Marty's body. It didn't matter that he was in a chair and not walking toward him. To Quinn, Marty was gorgeous, and every time he moved his arms and flexed his chest to propel his chair, Quinn imagined a cat prowling closer and closer to him, the way one of Wally's tigers stalked its prey.

"Are you waiting for me?" Marty asked with a grin.

"Oh, yeah," Quinn answered. Damn, he looked amazing when he smiled, and Quinn was pretty sure Marty was flirting with him, because he sure as hell was flirting with Marty. Quinn opened the door and then lifted Marty out of his chair, but didn't put him in the truck right away. He held him close to his body and leaned in close. Marty wrapped his arms around Quinn's neck and kissed him right there at the edge of the parking lot. Quinn held him tight, kissing Marty the way he'd been kissed the night before. His mind quickly began to center on every movement Marty made in his arms, and Quinn had to remember where they were. Once Marty stopped to breathe, Quinn carefully set him on the seat. "If I don't stop now, I won't be able to," Quinn managed to say, still short of breath as he closed the door and walked around the truck.

Quinn sucked in the cold air, trying to clear his lust-clouded head. He had to get himself under control. Yes, he wanted to spend time with Marty, but he didn't want to rush him, and he wondered if he was letting his tendency to fall too far too fast to get the better of him. "Fuck it," he whispered to himself. Quinn knew that all this was over as soon as Marty's family learned about him and about the ranch. They'd swoop in like some sort of posse to pull their son out of this den of iniquity. He had little doubt of that, and yes, he was probably moving too fast, but he reminded himself that he wasn't alone.

Pulling open the driver's door, Quinn looked at Marty, who smiled at him brightly, but the grin faded as Quinn climbed inside. "What's wrong?"

"Nothing," Quinn said, pulling the door closed. "I tend to get a little excited and sort of rush ahead without thinking." Quinn stared out the windshield.

"So you lead with your heart," Marty said softly. "There are worse things. Like walling it off so no one can reach it. Maybe you got hurt because of it, but at least you can feel. I've been scared to feel anything for another guy because of how my family might feel about it." Marty flipped the bird out the front window. "Well, screw them. I can't live for them or anyone else, and for your information, I may not be able to walk, but that doesn't mean I don't know my own mind or what I want. If I wasn't interested in you, I wouldn't have kissed you."

"I know," Quinn said. "I never thought that about you. I'm just a little scared."

"So am I," Marty said. "I'm scared I may never walk again, and I'm scared that I may have another stroke and end up back in the hospital, only this time I'll end up as some vegetable who can't even feed himself. But I'm not scared to feel something for someone else, not any longer. I spent days worrying about how I felt about you because it would hurt my family."

Quinn swallowed hard before turning to look at Marty. It was obvious from the set of his jaw and the intensity in his eyes that he meant what he was saying, at least for now. Quinn wasn't sure what to say, but he smiled and reached across the seat to take

Marty's hand. Marty squeezed in return, and then Quinn pulled his hand away so he could start the truck before driving back out toward the ranch. After pulling to a stop at the ranch, Quinn's phone rang.

"Wally says you're moving into the bunkhouse and need some help with your horses," Haven said as soon as Quinn answered. "Couldn't take your old man anymore?"

"That sums it up pretty well," Quinn admitted.

"Don't blame you one bit," Haven said, and Quinn could tell he was smiling. "I have some things to finish in the east range and then I'll be by in about an hour. How many horses are we transporting?"

"Two," Quinn answered, feeling a bit uneasy. "Dad tried to give me a hard time about them last night. He actually said they were his because he paid for the feed or some such crap." Quinn felt Marty's hand on his and some of the tension drained out of him at the simple touch.

"Then we'll go get them as soon as I can get there. Do you want to meet there?"

"Marty and I are at Dakota's," Quinn said, smiling across the seat at Marty. "He just got done with his therapy."

"Then I'll meet you there, and we can ride over together," Haven said before ending the call. Quinn put the phone back in his pocket and got out of the truck. After retrieving Marty's chair from the back, he helped him out of the truck, and damn, if he didn't want to carry him into the house and right into Marty's bedroom. He'd carry Marty for the rest of his life if it meant he could have him in his arms.

Reluctantly, Quinn set Marty in his chair. "I'll see you later," Quinn said, and Marty grinned before wheeling himself up the ramp and in the front door. He wanted to follow, but they both had work to do. Quinn got the truck unloaded and unpacked some of his things into his new room in the bunkhouse. Once that was done, he worked in the clinic for a while. It was his job to see that Wally had everything he needed when he needed it, and Quinn took that responsibility very seriously. When he was done, he walked through the barn and heard a truck pull into the drive.

"Are you ready to go?" Haven called from outside. Quinn picked up his pace and hurried around to the passenger door. Haven pulled the truck and horse trailer in a wide circle, and they began the trip to Quinn's father's house. "So I understand you and Marty are seeing each other."

"Yes. I really like him." Quinn couldn't stop a smile.

"Are you sure you know what you're getting into? You know who his father is?" Haven asked his questions cautiously.

"Yes," Quinn answered, shifting in his seat. "Would you have let that stop you and Phillip?"

Haven thought for a split second and shook his head. "Not for a second," Haven answered with a chuckle. "Sounds like you've got it bad."

"That's what scares me," Quinn admitted as Haven turned the corner. The truck sped up on the clear road and they picked up speed. "I know he isn't going to stay."

"I didn't think Phillip would, either. But things change, and sometimes you get lucky," Haven said. Quinn could only hope. They rode quietly for most of the rest of the way before pulling into his dad's drive and driving right up to the barn. No one seemed to be around, and Quinn was grateful for small favors as he pulled the barn door open. Four large heads appeared out of their stalls, curious about what was going on. "Which two are we taking?"

Quinn stroked the nose of each of his horses and sighed. "Largo and Hugh are mine." Quinn looked at the other two horses in the barn. "I wish I could take them all. Goodness knows my dad won't take proper care of them." Quinn wished he dared to simply take all four of them, but his dad would probably call the sheriff, and Quinn didn't have a leg to stand on.

"I'll get these two loaded while you get your saddles and tack," Haven said, and Quinn went into the tack room, lifting Largo's saddle off the tree and then carrying it out to the truck and putting it in the back. He went back inside and was bringing out the second one when he saw his dad pull into the drive. Quinn set the saddle down and waited as Haven led the first horse out of the barn.

"What do you think you're doing? I told you about taking them horses," his father said as he got out of the truck. "Largo is the best bloodline we have," his father explained, "and I'm not letting him go."

"You don't have a choice," Haven said before walking the horse up the ramp and into the trailer. Quinn stared at his father in silent rage until Haven returned. "The horses are his, and he has the paperwork to prove it."

"I'm calling the sheriff," his father said and pulled out his phone.

"You do that," Quinn said before turning to Haven. "Load the other horse." He'd had it with his father. "You haven't taken care of any of the horses in years, you lazy son of a bitch. All you want me around for is to clean up after you. Well, I'm done." Quinn turned away and got the last of his tack. He heard his father making his phone call, and by the time he had everything in the truck, he saw a sheriff's vehicle pull into the drive.

"What's going on?" the deputy asked as he strode toward them.

"He's stealing my horses," Quinn's father said, and Quinn rolled his eyes.

"The horses are mine and I have paperwork." Quinn pulled the papers out of his pocket and handed them to the deputy, who looked them over and then handed them back.

"What kind of trouble are you trying to cause, Lyle?" The deputy asked.

"He may have paperwork for the horses, but he also took saddles and tack," his father said with a self-satisfied smirk. What a total ass.

"Why are you being this way to your own son?" the deputy asked, but Quinn's dad remained silent, crossing his arms. "Do you have paperwork for the saddles and tack?" the deputy asked as he turned to Quinn.

"No, but they're mine. I bought them with my own money," Quinn said, a queasy feeling rising in his stomach.

The deputy walked around to the back of Haven's truck, where he looked at the saddles and lifted the tack. "You're saying this is yours?" the deputy asked his dad, and Lyle stuck out his chin defiantly. "Because I've known you for ten years, and you're the cheapest bastard I've ever met. This is good equipment, and I highly doubt you bought it." The deputy turned to Quinn. "I don't know what you did to piss him off, but I suggest you get the rest of your things."

"He's afraid that people will find out I'm gay," Quinn said before turning to go inside. He made his way to his room and got the last of his things, and then carried them to the truck. Quinn put them in the back, and he and Haven got ready to leave. The deputy got back into his car, following them as they slowly made their way down the drive and out to the road. As they made the turn, Quinn looked out the side window at the home he was leaving behind. "How could my own dad treat me like that?" Quinn muttered softly.

"You know what my dad tried to do to me," Haven said, and Quinn nodded. "The man was a total bastard and tried to steal the ranch from under me, taking advantage of being my trustee." Haven sighed softly. "Not all of us get a dad like Dakota's."

"Tell me about it," Quinn said, turning around to see the house disappear in the distance.

"You're better off away from him. I know it's hard to leave, but you'll feel better once you're around people who support you," Haven told him. Quinn knew the ranch foreman was right, but that didn't make the hurt any easier to take. He should have known his father would put up some sort of stink. He was definitely lazy and selfish.

Haven drove carefully and pulled slowly into Wally and Dakota's drive, trying not to jostle the trailer too much. He pulled as close to the barn as he could and then stopped. Quinn got out of the truck to help Haven unload the horses. It didn't take too long to get both horses settled in stalls and the tack put away. Quinn then carried the last of his stuff into the bunkhouse before thanking Haven for all his help. "Don't let your dad get you down," Haven said as he tugged Quinn into a hug. "He's the one losing something important." Quinn nodded and swallowed around the emotion that welled up from inside. "I need to get back to the guys, but it's going to be okay." Haven patted his shoulder lightly before getting back in the truck, and after turning around, he headed down the drive.

Quinn stood, half watching Haven go as he lost himself in his thoughts. The sound of the front door of the house banging closed caught his attention. Quinn turned as Marty glided down the ramp, propelling himself to where Quinn stood. "How did it go?"

Quinn shrugged. "My father was an ass, but the horses are in the barn," Quinn explained as Dolly loped up. Quinn scratched behind her ears, and then Maxine joined them. She glommed onto

Marty, and as Quinn watched, the large dog placed her front paws on Marty's knees before leaning in to give his face a good licking. Quinn laughed as Marty moved his face from side to side, Maxine following his every move as she proceeded to give Marty a good tongue bath. *Lucky dog.* "Maxine," Quinn scolded, and she looked toward him before plopping back onto the ground and bounding to Quinn for some attention. "Sorry," Quinn told Marty, who was wiping his face on his sleeve with a smile.

"She's affectionate," Marty said, and Quinn howled with laughter.

"She's a menace with her tongue, but she's still a good girl, aren't you?" Quinn talked to both of them for a few moments. When he stopped, they bounded off toward the barn, and Quinn stepped closer to Marty. "How was your morning?"

"Fine. I'm a little sore from therapy. I read to Jefferson until he fell asleep, and then I thought I heard you out here," Marty said, and Quinn leaned down, giving Marty a soft kiss.

"Let's get inside. It's getting colder, and I think we're probably in for some more snow." Spring was always like that—days of melting followed by more snow. "I'm going to check on things in the barn and then I'll be in." Quinn kissed Marty again and then hurried away. He made a quick run to check that all the horses had food and water before making sure Wally's extra travel cases were packed and ready. For some reason, bad weather always brought in a rash of birthing. While he was finishing up, Wally came in from his call, explaining that the horse he was called to see had been worse than expected. Quinn checked Wally's cases and refilled what had been used before setting both full sets on the table in preparation for the next call.

"Are the horses getting settled in?" Wally asked as they walked back though the barn.

"Yes," Quinn answered.

"I take it things didn't go well," Wally observed, and Quinn nodded his answer. Wally didn't press, and they both walked toward the house as the first large flakes of snow began to fall.

Inside the warm house, Quinn helped Wally make a quick lunch and then poked his head into Jefferson's room, where Marty sat next to the bed, reading quietly out loud while Jefferson appeared to be dozing. Marty stopped reading, and Jefferson didn't stir, so he marked his page and closed the book, quietly setting it on the table before gliding toward the door and out of the room.

They ate soup and sandwiches for lunch as the wind whistled around the house, blowing the snow in curtains of white. As Quinn had thought, Wally received a call about a horse in trouble, and Quinn went with him to help out.

They spent hours trying to get the foal to turn inside the mother, who lay on her side panting for breath. Quinn knew from the look on Wally's face that he was about to give up hope when the foal finally decided to turn, and whoosh, he slipped from his mother in a rush of horse and fluid, with Mr. Milford smiling and shaking both their hands. They washed up, and then Quinn got everything together while Wally took care of business, and soon they were on their way back to the ranch, driving in a full-on blizzard, the wind threatening to blow them off the road more than once. Quinn could barely see the road at times, and it was only the wind blowing the pavement clean on occasion that allowed them to find their way.

"I'd go back, but I'd probably end up in the ditch if I tried to turn around," Wally said, and Quinn agreed, keeping his eyes on the road to help Wally navigate. Quinn's legs shook with nervous energy, and by the time Wally pulled into the drive at the ranch, his knuckles were white from gripping the wheel. Wally pulled to a stop next to Dakota's truck, and they both got out. Quinn took the cases to the clinic and grabbed the full ones, carrying them into the house with him so they would be ready just in case Wally got another call.

Dakota met them at the door, a relieved expression on his face, and he immediately pulled Wally into his arms. Quinn heard the *humpf* as Wally was kissed right there. "You scared the hell out of me. They're saying this is the worst visibility in years and telling everyone not to drive." Wally seemed happy to let his big cowboy doctor envelop him in his arms. Quinn stepped by them and let them have their moment together. After taking off his coat, he hung it up and then joined Marty and Jefferson in the living room. They were watching golf on television, and it seemed out of place in contrast to the wind and snow whipping and whirling outside the windows.

Dakota and Wally joined them, and as soon as they sat down, Wally's phone rang. Dakota growled, and Wally lightly slapped his shoulder as he fished it out of his pocket. "What's going on, Wilson?" Wally listened for a while. "Sounds like colic again. The best thing you can do is walk him. I'd suggest up and down the center of the barn. Keep him moving and things will work themselves out. If it doesn't get better, call me." Wally listened for a few more minutes and then hung up. "Poor Wilson," Wally said as he stuffed his phone away again.

Quinn settled on the sofa next to Marty and held him close, letting his warmth soak though his still-cold clothes. Quinn closed his eyes and felt Marty put his arm around him "You smell nice," Quinn told Marty softly, resting his head against Marty's side. The wind kept picking up, howling around the house. Quinn was glad they were all inside and hoped the storm wouldn't last too long. Then everything went dark as the power died.

"I'll start the generator," Dakota said, stepping away from Wally.

"Do you need some help?" Quinn asked.

"No. It's all fueled up and shouldn't take too long to start," Dakota answered as he pulled on his coat, hat, and gloves. He looked like a mountain man as he walked out the back door. Quinn moved closer to Marty as the wind continued howling. He knew the temperature in the house hadn't begun to drop in the past five minutes, but it seemed colder. Against the sound of the wind, Quinn heard an engine start and then the lights came on again. Wally went around the house turning off everything except the lights in the room they were in. "There isn't enough power to run everything, so we need to be careful." Wally did leave the television on for Jefferson, but he turned off almost everything else. Wally left the room as Dakota came back inside. He returned with blankets, and Quinn snuggled under one of them with Marty while Wally draped one over Jefferson, and once Dakota had gotten out of his coat and built a fire, the two of them curled together under a blanket of their own.

The rest of the afternoon passed, broken by the sound of the wind, the crackle of the fire, and the drone of the television. Late in the afternoon, Dakota left to add more fuel to the generator. A phone rang, and Wally answered it.

"Goodness no, Liam. Stay where you are. I'll take care of the cats. You stay safe and warm, and I'll see you tomorrow." Wally hung up and dressed warmly. Quinn did as well, and after offering to help, he followed Wally to where he kept the meat for the cats. They prepared the cats' dinner and then together they trudged through the blowing snow to the cages where the cats lived. Quinn held the trays, and Wally dropped the meat into the cages. Each cat came out of his shelter and dragged the food back inside.

"They're certainly beautiful," Quinn shouted over the wind as they fed the last of the animals before heading back inside.

"Yes, they are," Wally agreed before motioning toward the second set of cages. Quinn nodded, and they trudged on, feeding the second set of large cats before hurrying as fast as they could back toward the house. Their footsteps had been obliterated by the wind, and from the cages, Quinn could barely see the house.

Keeping his face out of the wind, Quinn made his way back toward the house, the thick, wet snow sticking to his coat and pants, quickly soaking the fabric. Thankfully, it wasn't a long walk, and they made it back, holding the door so the wind didn't catch it. Once inside, they stomped the snow off their boots and then took off their wet things. As quickly as it had come up, the wind seemed to settle down some, and the fierce gusts seemed to level off into a steady wind that Quinn knew would probably blow all night. "Thank God it isn't bitter cold, just wet," Wally said as he hung up his coat. Quinn joined Marty on the sofa once again.

"Will you need to tend the generator all night?" Quinn asked.

Dakota nodded. "It has enough fuel to last about twelve hours right now, and I have a reserve tank for six additional hours. After that, we'll be in the dark, but the power company will have service restored pretty soon. This happens sometimes, and they're really good about getting it restored."

Quinn heard Wally in the kitchen, and soon he brought in huge bowls of hot soup for everyone. It was perfect for a night like this, and they watched television together until the power flickered and the hum of the generator kicked off. That seemed to act as a signal, because Dakota wheeled his dad down the hall, presumably to help him into bed. Wally followed a short time later. "I should go out to the bunkhouse," Quinn said, getting ready to get up. Marty put his arms around Quinn's neck and pulled him into a kiss that curled Quinn's toes. Soft, needy lips pressed to Quinn's

"Please don't," Marty whispered before kissing him again, this time hard and with a force that Quinn wasn't expecting.

Marty took possession of his mouth, clearly communicating what he wanted with his lips and tongue. Fire spread throughout Quinn's body, and he shifted on the sofa, pressing against Marty as he wrapped him in his arms.

"Are you sure?" Quinn asked.

Marty stopped moving. "Are *you* sure?"

Quinn kissed Marty with the passion that sprang from deep inside him. "I've wanted to be with you since I saw you almost naked." Quinn's chuckles quickly turned to a groan as Marty brought their lips back together. "You're a beautiful man," Quinn added once they parted, nearly breathless.

"Even though I'm in the chair?" Marty asked.

Quinn stroked Marty's cheek. "The chair is just transportation, not an extension of the man in it." Quinn stood up and positioned Marty's chair near the sofa. After helping him transfer himself into it, Quinn pushed Marty down the hallway to his room, turning out the lights as they went and then closing the bedroom door behind them. Marty placed his chair next to the bed and shifted himself onto the mattress. Quinn saw Marty bite his lower lip nervously. "Have you been with anyone before?"

"Not really," Marty answered a bit shyly.

"We can take this as slow as you need to," Quinn said as Marty began opening the buttons on his shirt. Quinn stepped to the bed and gently stilled Marty's hands. "Let me," he said before sitting on the edge of the bed. Quinn simply looked at Marty, watching Marty's chest rising and falling, eyes wide with anticipation, lips parted, tongue licking them nervously. Quinn took Marty's hand and slowly caressed his skin. "You're a stunning man," Quinn told Marty as he leaned closer, touching their lips together.

Marty responded to Quinn immediately, wrapping his arms around Quinn's neck. Their kiss deepened quickly, and Quinn shifted slightly on the bed, so he was lying next to Marty. They pressed their bodies together, and Quinn felt Marty's jeans-encased cock slide along his hip. They continued kissing as Quinn opened the buttons of Marty's shirt, parted the fabric, and let his hands roam up and down the soft skin of Marty's side. Every touch seemed to send little shivers through Marty, and Quinn loved that he could make him that excited from only a touch.

"Are you okay?" Quinn asked after breaking an extended kiss. Marty touched his kiss-swollen lips and smiled, amazement dancing in his eyes. "I'm afraid to put too much weight on you."

"I won't break," Marty answered, and Quinn smiled as he tugged his shirt over his head. He knew getting undressed was going to be awkward for Marty, so he gently removed Marty's shirt, kissing and licking the exposed skin. Marty giggled and squirmed at first when Quinn ran his tongue around his small, pink nipples, but the giggles morphed into deep moans when Quinn sucked a little harder. The moans continued and became more intense when Quinn licked his way down Marty's belly. He teased, licked, and kissed the soft, smooth, pale skin until Marty begged him to stop.

"I'm going to help you with the rest of your clothes," Quinn told Marty before removing his shoes and socks, letting them fall to the floor. Quinn caressed Marty's feet and legs before opening his pants and then gently tugging them off.

Marty wore magnificently tented white briefs, and Quinn longed to pull them away so he could taste Marty completely. But first he slid off the bed and toed off his shoes. Then he opened his pants and stepped out of them, standing still near the bed. Marty reached over and lightly caressed his stomach and chest. Quinn moved closer and closed his eyes. He wanted nothing more than to have Marty touch him. Quinn heard the bed creak, and then he was being held around the waist, Marty's cheek resting on his belly. Quinn held Marty lightly and felt warm, soft lips kissing his skin.

Marty caressed his back before sliding his hands down to his butt, pushing Quinn's underwear lower and lower. "I've dreamed for years about being with another man like this," Marty said, his breath flowing warmly over Quinn's skin. He continued pushing Quinn's briefs lower until his cock sprang free. After Marty's admission regarding his inexperience, Quinn expected Marty to be reticent. He wasn't. Quinn gasped as Marty slowly took his cock between his lips. Without thinking, Quinn rested his hands on Marty's head.

"Take it easy," he soothed, and then he gasped when Marty took him deep. Marty immediately backed off, but then took him again. Finessed, Marty wasn't, but Quinn didn't care in the least. After a few minutes, Quinn moved away, settling Marty back onto the bed before working the last of their clothing off.

Quinn stood by the side of the bed, looking at Marty in all of nature's glory. "You are so beautiful," Quinn said with a catch in his throat. Marty definitely was. His eyes sparkled with excitement, even in the dimness. His skin was light, but flawless, and it was readily apparent that up until a few months ago, he'd been an athlete in supreme shape, because even now, there were lines of muscle on his belly, and he had a strong chest and shoulders. Marty's legs were thin, and Quinn knew that was from lack of use. Reaching out, he stroked along one of Marty's thighs and felt him pull away slightly. "There's nothing to be ashamed of or self-conscious about," Quinn said as he continued to stroke up and down Marty's thigh.

"I can't do much with them," Marty said, lifting his right leg fairly well. He lifted his left leg some, but it shook, and he dropped it back onto the bed. He turned his head away, and Quinn leaned close.

"It doesn't matter to me if you're ever able to walk again. I mean, it won't make a difference in how I feel," Quinn said.

Marty rolled his head on the pillow, and Quinn leaned close, kissing him hard to emphasize what he'd said. Without thinking, he shifted onto the bed, covering Marty's body with his own.

Quinn groaned softly as he felt Marty's skin against his, hip to hip, chest to chest. Slowly, Marty rocked beneath him, moaning softly. Quinn kissed Marty deeply as he rolled them on the mattress. Marty gasped softly, and Quinn smiled up at him as he gave Marty control. Quinn stroked down Marty's back as Marty lifted himself up slightly. "Take all the time you want," Quinn said, and Marty smiled a mischievous grin. Quinn steadied Marty by cupping his butt, arching his back when Marty sucked on one of his nipples.

"You taste like fresh air," Marty told him, and Quinn felt Marty flex his hips, sliding his cock along Quinn's hip.

"And you taste like sunshine on a summer day," Quinn said, kissing Marty deeply, flexing his own hips. He kept time with Marty, sliding his cock against incredibly warm skin. Marty made a steady stream of little noises that blended with the sound of the wind outside the house until it too seemed to join in their lovemaking.

"Marty," Quinn gasped softly, cupping his cheeks and bringing their lips together as he felt Marty tense, and then searing heat spread between them. Quinn watched Marty's blissful expression as he came, making the most wonderful sexy mewling noises Quinn had ever heard.

Quinn was so enthralled in Marty's reaction that he completely forgot about himself. He'd never done that before. Carefully, he caressed Marty's cheek before lightly tugging him into a kiss. Marty continued moving above him and Quinn took the hint, grinding his hips upward as the slickness between them spread. Pressure rapidly built inside him, and within a matter of seconds, Quinn's eyes slid closed and his mouth gaped open as he came hard and fast, adding his own release to Marty's.

"Wow, that was sexy," Marty whispered, and Quinn slid his eyes open, trying to catch his breath. "I've never seen that before."

"You never watched yourself?" Quinn asked, and Marty shook his head slowly. Quinn imagined Marty coloring. "Are you blushing?" Marty answered with a nod. After what they'd just done, it was the thought of watching himself that had made Marty blush. The man was totally adorable. "Nothing to be ashamed of, but you've missed one of the most amazing sights ever."

Marty looked away, and Quinn touched his chin, bring their gazes back together before kissing Marty's sweet lips. "But…."

Quinn helped Marty settle on his back on the bed. "But what?" Quinn prompted, but Marty seemed to clam up. Quinn got up and used some tissues to clean them both before rejoining Marty on the bed. "Just tell me what you're thinking," Quinn said.

"Was what we did wrong?"

"No, it wasn't," Quinn answered definitively. He had no doubt about that. It had taken him quite some time, but he'd finally arrived at that conclusion, and after seeing Wally and Dakota together, he'd become firm in his conviction.

"How do you know?" Marty asked quietly.

"Did we hurt anyone, including each other?" Quinn asked, and Marty shook his head. "Have you seen Wally and Dakota together and have you ever seen two people more in love in your life?"

"But… they're different," Marty said, and Quinn pulled him close.

"No, they're not. They're two people who happen to have been lucky enough to have met their soul mate—nothing more, nothing less. There's too much harshness and closed-mindedness in this world, and we can't listen to it. Love isn't wrong, period. No matter what anyone may say or what they may use to try to justify hate and bigotry, loving someone is never wrong." Quinn could almost see the questions running behind Marty's eyes, and he kissed away any other queries he might have had. There were so many he didn't know the answer to, or wasn't ready to provide an answer for, that avoidance was his only choice. "What's right and wrong for you is for you to decide, not anyone else," Quinn whispered as he broke the kiss, settling on the mattress as he pulled Marty to him. Slowly Marty rolled onto his side, and Quinn helped with the bedding. Eventually he was spooned to Marty's back, arm around his chest, blankets pulled up tight around them. Quinn could hear Marty's breathing begin to even out and he knew the beautiful man in his arms was falling asleep.

As Quinn closed his eyes, he felt Marty take his hand. "I think you're right," Marty mumbled, and other than the sound of the wind, those soft words were the last thing Quinn heard until morning.

Chapter Six

"OKAY, let's take one more trip down the bars," Johnny said, though Marty's arms felt ready to give out.

"You're a real sadist," Marty griped, but he turned around and slowly forced his legs to move. It still felt as though he were trying to send the signals to his legs through a bowl of pudding, but if he thought hard enough, he could get them to move.

"You can do this," Johnny said, standing at the far side of the bars. "Maybe if I got Quinn to stand here making kissy noises, you'd try harder." Johnny could be such a tease, but Marty smiled anyway.

"Shut up," he retorted and looked down to lift his foot.

"Look ahead, not at your feet. Your brain needs to create the new pathway, and it doesn't go through your eyes. I know it seems harder, but in the long run you'll progress faster if you can lift your leg without looking."

Marty swore and looked at Johnny, forcing his legs to move. "You… are… one… mean… bastard," Marty grunted as he took each baby step.

"Maybe, but you made it," Johnny said with a smile before helping Marty into his chair. "You did good today," Johnny told him with a smile, and Marty used all his restraint to keep from flipping him off. His legs hurt, his arms ached, and he was breathing like a racehorse after a hard run. But Johnny was right—he had made it, and more than once, which was an improvement.

"Why is it taking so long?" Marty asked as he slowly wheeled himself toward the door.

Johnny followed behind him. "The stroke did a number on the part of your brain that controls your motor skills." Johnny leaned against the desk while Marty pulled on his coat. "Sometimes when part of the brain is damaged, a whole new section takes over for it, and I think that's probably what's happening with you. That's a good thing, but it also takes time and hard work. You can't rush it. We've talked about injuries, and that's exactly what will happen if we push too hard." Johnny pushed himself away from the desk. "So to change the subject, tell me how things are going with your cowboy lover."

"Quinn is Wally's assistant," Marty corrected.

"The man rides and works at the ranch too, doesn't he?" Marty nodded. "Then he's a cowboy, and everyone knows cowboys are sexy as hell, so spill." Johnny's eyes actually widened in anticipation. "Come on," he coaxed.

"The last three weeks have been great," Marty answered, moving closer to the door.

"I take it he hasn't been spending much time in the bunkhouse over those three weeks." Johnny grinned when Marty blushed. "I thought so." Marty looked away. "A happy patient is a healthy patient, so whatever you two are doing seems to be working." Johnny patted his shoulder. "Besides, everyone knows cowboys make the best rides."

Marty felt his surliness slip away as he laughed out loud. "Where do you come up with this stuff?" Marty asked as he headed for the door. He had to get out of here before his sex life was completely dissected. "I'm not saying you're wrong, I'm just curious about all these sayings you have." Marty pulled open the door just in time, as Quinn hurried in.

"Hi, cutie," Quinn said as he leaned down for a kiss. "I have to get back to the ranch, so let's ride."

Johnny waited two seconds before he started laughing, and Marty tried to keep a straight face, but failed miserably.

"What's so funny?" Quinn asked, looking at both of them.

"Nothing," Marty said quickly and headed for the door.

"A dirty mind is a terrible thing to waste," Johnny called as the door swung closed behind them.

"Ignore him," Marty said as he hurried to where Quinn had parked the truck. Spring was finally starting to look like it was going to stick around. Some of the trees were showing their first buds, and a few early flowers even lined the walk as Marty approached the truck. There was still a definite nip in the air, but the sun felt warm on his skin, and he couldn't help stopping for a few moments to enjoy it. But he knew Quinn was in a bit of a rush, so he continued on.

Quinn helped him into the truck, and soon they were on their way to the ranch. Marty told him all about therapy, babbling for most of the trip. As Quinn made one of the turns, Marty's phone rang and he fished it out of his pocket. "Hi, Mom," Marty said brightly. "How are you?"

"Good," she answered. "You hadn't called in a few days, and I thought I'd see how you were doing."

"I'm fine," Marty said and relayed the details of the therapy session. "It's taking some time, but I'm able to walk with help. I can't support my own weight yet, but Johnny says that's a matter of time."

"That's excellent, honey," she said and then paused. "I know you're busy, but I thought I'd drive over to see you this weekend. It's been over a month, and I miss you."

"I miss you too," Marty said, swallowing around the panic that threatened to overtake him. He had known he could only put off his mother for so long before her curiosity and motherly meddling took over.

"I thought I'd drive over on Friday. Cassie wants to come too, so I was wondering if there was a nice hotel nearby that we could stay in. Your brother is going to stay home with your father and they're going to have a weekend together, so it'll just be Cassie and me. Do you know if there's a spa nearby?"

Marty laughed, and a bit of the tension that had been building slipped away. "This is a ranching community. They don't have things like spas here. The town isn't that big, but there's a beauty parlor."

His mother began to chuckle. "I was kidding," she said, continuing to laugh. "When have you ever known me to be a spa person?"

"It's good to hear you happy, Mom," Marty said, but in the back of his mind he wondered how happy she was going to be when she found out about him and the guys on the ranch. At least she was staying at a hotel, and he could probably limit the amount of time she actually spent at the ranch with the guys.

"I could say the same. You've sounded different the last few weeks," she said. Marty heard voices behind her, and she shifted the phone. "I'll see you early Friday evening. Call me with the hotel details and directions."

"I will," he agreed, and she said good-bye before hanging up. Marty disconnected as well and then shoved the phone in his pocket.

"Was that your mom?" Quinn asked, and Marty nodded. "I take it she's coming for a visit."

"This weekend," Marty said as butterflies whipped up in his stomach with a vengeance. "She and Cassie will be here on Friday. I need to get a hotel room for them." Marty was already planning the weekend in his head. He'd meet his mother and sister at the hotel and the three of them would go to dinner at the steak house. They'd talk for a while, and then he'd get a ride back to the ranch and they'd go to bed. That was Friday, easy as pie. Saturday was going to be more difficult because they'd want to see the ranch and meet the people he worked with, but even then he could minimize the amount of time they were actually at the ranch by showing them around town. Although if he knew Cassie, she'd definitely want to see Wally's cats, but he could arrange for that. They'd be visiting on Saturday during the day, so most of the guys would be working. He could introduce his mother to Jefferson. Maybe he could also arrange for her to meet Johnny. His mother would love to meet his therapist and hear from him about his progress.

"Do you want me to meet them, or should I make myself scarce?" Quinn asked, and Marty opened his mouth to ask him to keep himself as busy as possible, but the words wouldn't come out, especially not when he saw the hurt in Quinn's eyes.

"I want you to meet them," he answered, knowing he would probably come to regret that decision. Marty reached across the seat, and Quinn took his hand. "I'll have to introduce you as a friend."

"I know," Quinn said, and Marty could feel the tension building in the air. "I know how you feel and who your family are, but please be yourself and try not to worry. We all live in Wyoming, and in case you haven't noticed, in public, we act like everyone else. Besides, it isn't as though there's a sign out front that says 'Wally and Dakota's Big Gay Ranch'." They both chuckled for a second, but the mirth didn't last long.

Marty sighed. "I wish things could be different."

"So do I," Quinn said as he made the turn into the ranch drive. He pulled up near the house. Marty leaned across the seat, hoping for a kiss, but Quinn opened his door and got out. Marty opened his door, and Quinn brought around his chair and helped him into it.

"Quinn, it's just for a day or so," Marty said, and he saw Quinn nod and swallow. He waited to see what Quinn would do and was relieved when Quinn leaned forward for a light kiss. Marty smiled and made his way toward the barn so he could make sure all the horses were set. Once he was done, he wheeled himself into the house, and after taking off his coat, went into Jefferson's room. He picked up the book and then stopped, looking into Jefferson's eyes. "My mother is coming for a visit this weekend."

"You knew she would," Jefferson said, his voice more slurred than usual, and Marty reached to the tray for some water. He held the straw for Jefferson, who took a small drink. "Beer would taste better," Jefferson said, and Marty smiled. "So how are you going to handle this?" Jefferson sounded a little more understandable.

"Keep them as busy as possible," Marty answered.

"Are you going to introduce her to Quinn?" Jefferson asked.

"Yes. I'm not going to hide him." At least he'd made that decision.

"You know your mother may like him, and it's harder to dismiss someone you know," Jefferson offered. Marty knew he was right, but he could not shake his feeling of impending doom. "Most of the time, what we fear is worse than reality." Jefferson lifted his head off his pillow, staring into Marty's eyes. "The important thing is to treat Quinn nicely. Your mother doesn't have to know what he means to you if you aren't ready to tell her, but don't ignore him or treat him badly. If you're going to introduce him as your friend, then treat him like one and not some dirty little secret." That was the most that Marty had heard Jefferson say at one time, and Jefferson continued staring at Marty.

"Okay," Marty agreed, even though he was scared to death. "I feel like such a coward for not telling her." Jefferson kept quiet, and Marty knew he wasn't going to answer because that decision couldn't come from someone else. After looking through the pages of the book, Marty found where he'd left off and began to read, losing himself in the story for a while.

MARTY had been nervous all day. He'd already cleaned and straightened the room he was using, in case his mother wanted to see it. At therapy that morning, he'd been distracted, and Johnny had pushed him harder than usual. Once the self-imposed torture was over, Quinn had picked him up like he usually did, but they hadn't talked much on the way back. Marty knew that was largely his fault. His tension and nervousness seemed to be rubbing off on everyone at the ranch. After checking his room over one last time, Marty made sure his clothes looked neat before wheeling himself out to the living room. He'd been waiting for his mother to call for a while now, and finally his phone rang.

"We're about half an hour away," his mother said excitedly.

"Then I'll meet you at the hotel," he said, getting ready to ask Quinn for a ride.

"Don't bother—we have the address for the ranch and the GPS will get us there just fine. We'll see you in a little while." She sounded excited as she ended the call, and Marty thought he might to be ill right there.

"Do you need a ride?" Quinn asked, and Marty shook his head.

"She's coming here," he explained.

"It's going to be fine," Quinn told him. Marty wasn't so sure. "Everyone knows you haven't told her, and no one is going to spill the beans. Coming out to your family is something you have to do in your own time. We all feel that way, so relax and enjoy the time with your mother and sister."

Marty looked up at Quinn from his chair. "What did I do to deserve this kind of understanding? I thought you'd be angry with me." The truth was, he was angry with himself that he didn't have the nerve to say something.

"What would happen if you told her when she arrived?" Quinn asked softly.

Marty thought for a second as a shudder went through him. "Honestly? She'd probably get back in the car and drive home as fast as she could. But not before packing all my things and bundling me into the backseat, even if she had to carry me over her shoulder. Then she'd call my father, and the yelling and screaming would begin and continue the entire drive home. And once we got there, my parents would try their best to convince themselves, and me, that somehow Wally and Dakota had turned their precious son gay." Marty felt his stomach bounce at the thought. "Maybe I should go home with them when they leave. At least when they do find out, they wouldn't make trouble for everyone here."

"You asked how I can be understanding?" Quinn shrugged. "It's because I want you to stay. I know you aren't ready to deal with what's going to happen when you tell your folks. I hope you will be eventually, but I can give you some time. Telling my dad wasn't easy, and look how that turned out in the end." Quinn leaned closer. "Everything will be just fine." Quinn's phone rang, and he answered it, waving as he grabbed his coat and then hurried out of the house. Marty watched through the front window as Quinn jumped in his truck and was gone.

Marty stayed where he was, watching the road until he saw his mother's black Lincoln slow down and carefully pull into the drive. After putting on his coat, Marty pulled open the door and rolled out onto the front porch. Both his mother and his sister hurried away from the car and up onto the porch to bury him in hugs. Marty lifted Cassie onto his lap and gave her a ride back inside.

"This is very nice," his mother was saying as Marty led them into the living room.

"Everyone is pretty much out working right now. Mr. Holden is home, but he's sleeping. His nurse should be in soon, and then I can show you around the ranch a little bit."

"Where are the kitties?" Cassie asked, and Marty turned around and said, "Go into the kitchen and look out the back window. You'll see the cages back out under the tree. You can't go see them unless Wally is with you. They aren't pets." Cassie nearly ran out of the room, and Marty heard a chair move across the kitchen floor.

"How can they keep wild animals like that?" his mother asked a little judgmentally.

"Wally's a vet, and he rescues them. He told me he nurses them back to health and then tries to find them homes in zoos or captive breeding programs. Most of what he has are endangered species, and he's helping to preserve them." Marty tried to keep the touch of indignation he felt out of his voice.

"Have you seen them up close?" Cassie asked, running back into the room.

"No. It's been too wet, but once the ground dries out I should be able to go back to see them," Marty answered, and Cassie ran back into the kitchen, her ponytail bobbing behind her. Marty couldn't help wishing that he'd be able to run like that again someday. He sighed and turned his attention back to his mother.

"How is your therapy coming?" his mother asked, and Marty locked the wheels of his chair.

"Give me your hand," he told her, and she stepped next to him. Marty pushed himself up using the arms of the chair and then used his mother's arm to steady himself the rest of the way, until he was standing in front of the wheelchair.

"That's wonderful," she exclaimed, moving in her excitement, and Marty felt his balance start to go. Still holding his mother's arm tightly, he sat back down in the chair. "I was so afraid you wouldn't make much progress here." The "without me pushing you" part of that statement was left unsaid, but Marty understood it as clearly as if she'd actually said the words.

"I like it here, Mom. I have a job and things they expect me to do. I keep my room clean on my own. Help with Mr. Holden's care, feed and water the horses, sweep the barn, and when it gets drier, I'll be able to help with tasks outside. I feel useful here, like I'm really making a contribution."

His mother looked skeptical. "You're just doing simple jobs that you could do at home." She stood up and walked to the front window, peering out for a few moments before turning to look at him again. "How do you help with Mr. Holden's care?"

"I sit with him for part of the day, bring him things he needs, and read to him. Dr. Holden can't be home as much as he'd like, so I make sure Jefferson isn't alone when the nurse isn't here." Marty felt sadness wash over him. "Mom, he's dying."

"They told you that?" she asked, and Marty shook his head.

"No one had to tell me. I can see it. In the time I've been here, I can see him sleeping more and doing less. He gets quieter and tires more and more easily." Marty looked toward the hallway. "He knows it too; I know he does," Marty whispered. "He's one of the most amazing people I've ever met. When he's awake, we talk and he tells me stories about starting the ranch."

"Why doesn't his son stay with him?" she asked a bit haughtily.

"I asked Jefferson that, and he told me it's because he'd kill Dakota if he let his practice go. Mr. Holden told me that more than anything he wants Dakota to be happy. 'The proudest moment in my life was when I got to watch my son graduate from medical school.'" Marty mimicked Jefferson's voice. His mother simply nodded, and Marty thought she understood.

"I saw one of the tigers stretch in the cage. They're huge," Cassie said as she raced back into the room. She tried to jump on his lap, but Marty steadied her before carefully lifting her up. "I missed you," she said before turning to give Marty a hug.

"I missed you too," he said, returning her hug as the front door opened and Wally came in.

"Wally," Marty said when he entered the room. "This is my mother, Rowena Green. Mom, this is Wally Schumacher. He's a veterinarian."

"It's nice to meet you," Wally said, extending his hand. Marty's mother shook it. "Have we met?"

"Yes. Dakota and I met you and your husband a few years ago at a conference in Cheyenne about water-rights preservation. The senator was the featured speaker." Wally smiled, and surprisingly, so did his mother.

"So has my son been behaving himself?" she asked, sitting down in one of the chairs.

"Mom," Marty protested, and Wally winked at him quickly.

"Marty's been a big help. Jefferson loves him, and he's helped a lot around here," Wally said. "Please excuse me. I've been out on calls all afternoon and I need to clean up." Wally nodded graciously to Marty's mother and then left the room.

"Mom, we should get you and Cassie settled in your hotel, and then I thought we could go to dinner and talk for a while."

Marty knew everyone would begin getting home soon, and his mother would undoubtedly notice that there wasn't a single woman on the ranch.

"All right," she answered, and Marty saw her cover a small yawn with her hand. "It was a long ride, and I could use a chance to freshen up a bit." His mother stood up, gathered Cassie and her things, and they walked toward the door. Marty got his coat and followed her outside, and after transferring to the passenger seat, they stowed his chair behind him and headed into town.

Marty had never been so happy to be heading to a hotel in his life. At least the initial part of his mother's visit had gone well. Cassie asked all kinds of questions on the way to the hotel, mostly about the cats, and Marty answered what he could. "When I told Wally you were coming, he promised he'd take you to see them. So when you come to the ranch tomorrow, you can ask him."

"Okay," she agreed happily, and Marty gave his mother directions to the small hotel where he'd reserved a room.

"It isn't fancy, but is quite nice," Marty told his mother. "There weren't a lot of options."

"I'm sure it's just fine," she soothed, and she continued driving. The hotel was on the edge of town. There weren't a lot of rooms, and Marty had to wait in the lobby because his mother and sister's room was on the second floor and the elevator was out of order. The woman behind the counter apologized many times, but Marty said it was okay and settled in a corner of the cozy sitting room while his mother and sister went upstairs to clean up.

"Would you like some coffee?" the pleasant lady, who appeared to be about his mother's age, asked.

"That would be nice, thank you," Marty answered, and she brought him a mug and set it on the table near him.

"Is that your mother?" she asked, sitting in the chair nearest him, and Marty nodded. "I know her from somewhere, but I can't quite figure it out." Marty, of course, knew exactly where she'd seen her—on the news standing next to his father—but years of training had taught him to keep quiet. His family was public enough without all of them being recognized everywhere they went. That was why his mother often checked into hotels under her maiden name.

"The hotel is very nice," Marty complimented, changing the subject easily. It wasn't a lie. The entire place had been decorated with loving care, and it was obvious from the woman's smile that she'd done it all herself.

"You're very sweet, and I'm sorry I don't have a room on this floor," she told him with a smile, coloring slightly, and Marty smiled back as his right leg bounced up and down. "You nervous about something?" she asked, and Marty stopped his leg from moving.

"I'm just excited about seeing my mom and sister. It's been a month," he answered, but it wasn't exactly the truth. He was very nervous, and no matter what he did, he couldn't get those feelings to subside. He took a deep breath and let it out slowly and quietly, trying to calm his racing heart.

"Enjoy your visit with your family," the proprietress said before getting up as a young couple entered the hotel. They looked like they were in high school, and Marty listened as they were politely informed that the hotel was full for the evening.

Marty drank the strong coffee, draining the mug, and then he set it back on the table and waited for his mother and sister. He'd finished the coffee out of politeness, but now he wished he hadn't—it only seemed to make him even more jittery. His mother and sister came down a few minutes later, and Marty thanked the lady for the coffee, bringing her the mug with a smile. Then they drove to the nicest restaurant in town. The steakhouse was full, but thankfully they were seated right away, and some of Marty's nervousness faded to the background when he didn't see anyone he knew.

Dinner was very nice, and by the time it was over, Marty realized how much he'd missed his mother and sister. They talked about his therapy, Marty's dad's reelection campaign, and Cassie told Marty about her riding lessons and how she was going to be a great equestrian. By the time the meal was over, his mother looked tired and Cassie was half asleep, leaning against him at the table. His mother insisted on paying the bill, and then they left, with Marty holding his sister on his lap as he rolled out to the car. "Do you need me to drive you back to the ranch?"

"No. I texted a friend and he's going to pick me up in a few minutes. Just take Cassie back to the hotel, and I'll see you at the ranch in the morning," Marty said. His mother seemed relieved. She bundled Cassie into the car, and after giving him a hug and a kiss on the cheek, she left. Marty went back inside and waited until a familiar truck pulled into the lot. Rolling out, Quinn met him by the sidewalk. "Let me try," Marty told Quinn, who stayed close and was ready to help as Marty carefully stood up and for the first time transferred himself onto the seat of Quinn's truck. He sighed tiredly as he pulled the door closed. Marty heard Quinn place his chair in the back and then he opened the driver's door and climbed in with a huge grin.

"You did great," Quinn told him before starting the engine. "How did the visit with your mother go?"

"It was fine, but exhausting." Marty had no idea why he was so tired. He hadn't really done anything other than accompany his mother and sister to dinner, but he could barely keep his eyes open. "They're coming to the ranch tomorrow, and Cassie wants to see Wally's cats and Mom wants to meet everyone. She met Wally today, but she's excited to meet everyone else. I think she wants to make sure I'm behaving."

"You have most of the time, but somehow I don't think you will be tonight," Quinn told him mischievously, and Marty finally felt the knots that had been tied in his stomach begin to unwind. Marty spent much of the drive lost in thought, and Quinn seemed quiet as well. At the ranch, Quinn helped him out of the truck, and they went inside, where some sort of gathering seemed to be taking place. "Must be Wally and Dakota's turn at poker night," Quinn commented as he hung up the coats.

Marty knew most of the people, including Haven and Phillip, and Steven and Wilson. "I don't think you know Liam and Troy," Wally said, making introductions. The actual poker portion of the evening appeared to be over, and everyone was now talking, eating, and drinking either soda or coffee.

"I understand your mother's in town," Phillip said.

"Yes. I left her and my sister at the hotel," Marty answered, relaxing for the first time that day. "They'll be here sometime in the morning, if that's okay," Marty said, and both Wally and Dakota nodded. "Cassie wants to see the cats really badly."

"I'll take her to see them," Wally said.

"Does your mother know about you?" Phillip asked, and Marty shook his head. "You're kidding, right?" Phillip asked, and Wally whapped him on the shoulder.

"We didn't all come out of the womb in a feather boa and high heels, the way you did," Wally teased before looking around the room. "Each of us came to understand who we were in a different way, and it wasn't easy for any of us." Marty saw Dakota's gaze settle on Phillip. "Marty deserves the time we all had to decide who we were and to come out in our own time and at our own pace," Dakota said.

"I was just teasing," Phillip said quietly to Marty.

"It's okay," Marty said softly. "I've thought quite a few times that I should just tell her, but…."

Phillip stood up and walked over to where Marty was sitting. "All kidding aside, you need to do what your heart tells you. And if it tells you now isn't the time to come out to your folks, then don't. You have people here who care about you and accept you for who you are." To Marty's surprise, Phillip hugged him. "I know how hard it will be to have the talk with your parents, especially in light of the things your dad has been championing, so you do it when you feel confident you can handle the fallout."

Marty nodded, and Phillip moved away. Slowly, the conversation in the room returned to normal. Marty half listened and wondered if Phillip's phrasing had been accidental or deliberate, because his coming out could have repercussions and fallout far beyond his immediate family.

"Are you tired?" Quinn asked softly.

"Yes," Marty whispered in return as he removed the brakes from the wheels of his chair and slowly backed out of the room. Everyone said good night, and a few minutes later, Marty was in his bedroom with Quinn. The door was closed and the sounds from the living room muted so nothing specific could be heard. "I don't understand how you can be so patient with me," Marty said as he shifted from the chair to the bed.

"Hey," Quinn whispered as he stroked Marty's cheek. "There are times when I've wanted you to just tell your family and get it over with. I've wondered if maybe you're making too much of this, but then I remind myself that you being gay isn't my secret to tell—it's yours." Quinn sat on the edge of the bed. "You know you can't keep this a secret forever. Your family will eventually either find out or figure it out. Either way, it'd be better if you told them yourself."

Marty closed his eyes and sighed. "I know. I want to try to make it past the election. Then dad will have six more years, and while people may try to hold it against him, no one will remember any of it once the news story changes."

Quinn shifted on the mattress, pressing Marty back until his head rested on a pillow. "Are you really sure your family will react badly?"

"I don't know. But the things that will be said about me and everyone here will be mean-spirited and hurtful. According to my dad, his opponent in the primary is having difficulty getting traction because Dad's record is stellar. He's done a great job for Wyoming. But my coming out could be the issue he needs to press Dad on topics that none of us want pressed. Like the whole gay-marriage thing. The issue has died down and isn't really going anywhere, but if my dad has a gay son, then he's going to be pressed to push it again." Marty's head spun. "I don't want to talk about politics or my dad right now." Marty wound his arms around Quinn's neck, tugging him closer. Without saying anything more, Marty kissed Quinn hard enough that he might have tasted a bit of blood. "I need to be alone with you."

Quinn moved and Marty was pressed into the mattress. "Do you want me to make everything go away for a while?"

"Yes," Marty answered, and Quinn kissed him once again.

"Then let's get these clothes off," Quinn rasped, and in a matter of seconds, their clothes were in a pile on the floor and Quinn's naked body covered his. Marty sighed, holding Quinn tight as he was kissed possessively. For the past three weeks, whenever their bedroom door was closed, Quinn seemed to turn into one of Wally's tigers. Quinn grabbed Marty's wrists, pulling them up over his head. Without a word being said, Marty knew that he was to grasp the headboard. Quinn had done this many times before. At first, Marty had resisted, but Quinn had gently told him it was so he could have unfettered access to every part of Marty's body.

Quinn slithered down, kissing a trail down Marty's chest and stomach while he stroked Marty's skin. Marty shivered in the warm room and his head throbbed with excitement as Quinn lightly ran his hands down Marty's tender sides. He had to stop himself from trying to squirm away from the slightly ticklish touch. But as soon as Marty felt Quinn's lips on his cock, all other thoughts flew from his mind. Marty's breath quickened and his pulse raced in anticipation of Quinn's lips on him. "What do you want?"

"You already know," Marty gasped, moving his hips upward. He wasn't above begging and he thought he was going to have to, but then Quinn licked along his length like a lollipop, and Marty whimpered as his entire body began to shake. Nothing he'd ever experienced compared to what he felt when Quinn touched him—hands, tongue, lips, cock, it didn't matter. It was like Marty craved Quinn's touch any way he could get it.

"I love that sound you make," Quinn told him.

"What sound?" Marty asked, and then Quinn sucked the head of his cock into his mouth. The groan Marty made startled him, and he felt and heard Quinn hum around his cock.

"That sound," Quinn said, holding Marty's cock firmly in his hand before sucking him deep. Marty reacted from the tips of his toes to his ears. Every nerve in his body fired at the same time as Quinn's searing heat and pressure engulfed him. Marty gripped the bedding and clamped his eyes closed in an effort to keep himself from tumbling over the abyss of pleasure too soon. Quinn had barely touched him, and Marty could already feel his excitement bubbling up from what felt like the depths of his soul. "Too much?" Quinn asked as he pulled his mouth away.

Marty gasped and uncrossed his eyes, breathing shallowly through his excitement. "No," he lied, and Quinn chuckled.

"Okay, then," Quinn said right before sucking him to the root. Marty rolled his head on the pillow. It felt like Quinn was trying to suck his brains out through his dick, and Marty loved every minute of it. Clutching the sheets in his fist, Marty bucked his hips forward as best he could, holding on for dear life as Quinn sucked and licked Marty to heaven. Within seconds, Marty knew he was ready to scream as the pressure built to unbelievable heights. He brought his hand to his mouth, biting on the heel as he came in a blinding flash. Marty felt Quinn swallowing around him and he shook, the entire bed vibrating along with him.

Once the shakes subsided and Marty could breathe and think again, he felt Quinn's lips slide away from him. Soon Marty was being kissed, Quinn exploring Marty's mouth with his tongue, and Marty could taste himself on Quinn's lips. "What about you?" Marty managed to ask between gasping breaths, but all he got from Quinn were more kisses.

Beneath Quinn, Marty slowly rolled over, parted his legs, and waited. Soon he felt Quinn settle on top of him, but very little of his weight actually pressed onto Marty. "Are you sure?" Quinn whispered breathily in Marty's ear. Over the past weeks, they explored many things together, but an actual coupling, like Marty was hoping for, they hadn't done yet. Marty felt Quinn stroke up and down his back before cupping and kneading his butt.

"Yes, I'm sure," Marty said as he turned to look over his shoulder. Quinn leaned forward, kissing him hard and then nibbling his shoulder and down his back. Marty felt relaxed and almost sleepy under Quinn's gentle ministrations. When Quinn kissed his butt, Marty chuckled softly. The laughter turned to a soft moan as Quinn continued kneading his butt cheeks, kissing and then licking his skin. "What are you…?" Marty gasped and threw his head back when Quinn swept his tongue down his cleft and then teased the skin of his opening. Marty was about to protest that Quinn couldn't do that, but all he could do was groan deeply when Quinn's tongue seemed to work its way into his body. "Jesus!"

"You like that, don't you?" Quinn teased before licking him again. Marty arched his back, throwing his head back as Quinn completely blew his mind. He had no idea how long Quinn tongued him, but by the time he was done, Marty was as hot and sexy-feeling as he could ever remember being. It took him a few seconds to realize the sensation had stopped, and then he felt

Quinn slowly insert a slick finger into his body. Marty hadn't even heard Quinn open the drawer next to the bed, but when he glanced around, he saw the lube and a condom on the nightstand. He didn't have much time to look, because Quinn touched a spot inside him, and Marty shivered with excitement.

Marty groaned when Quinn slipped his fingers out of him. He felt Quinn's weight shift on the bed and then heard a package being ripped open. Marty tried to contain his excitement and waited. "Relax and breathe," Quinn said into his ear as Marty felt him press against his opening. "I'm going to go slow, but you have to promise you'll tell me if you want me to stop." Marty nodded and then he felt Quinn press into him.

At first nothing seemed to happen, but then Marty felt his body open up, and he gasped. The initial pressure and pain threatened to overwhelm him, and Quinn stopped moving. Marty breathed and waited, hoping it would pass, and within a few seconds, he felt the pain subside. Quinn pressed deeper, and Marty breathed as steadily as he could, and soon he felt Quinn's hips against his butt. Then, everything stopped. Marty felt Quinn's weight on him, and then, slowly, Quinn rolled them onto their sides and held him close. Marty could feel Quinn's breath on his skin as he throbbed deep inside his body. Each jump of Quinn's cock sent a thrill of desire through him. "I feel so full," Marty moaned, and Quinn tugged him closer.

Slowly, Quinn began to move, pulling out of Marty's body. Marty's breath caught, and Quinn stilled. "Is this okay?"

"God, yes," Marty moaned as Quinn pressed back into him, and began to move a little faster. "Please, Quinn," Marty begged, and Quinn continued his slow movements in and out of his body. Never had Marty dreamed that anything in this world could feel as wonderful as having Quinn inside him. Quinn held him close, moving their bodies slowly together as the world seemed to narrow to just the two of them. Everything that had worried Marty slipped away as Quinn made his body sing.

Marty wasn't too sure how he was going to last. The sensation was so intense, but when Quinn reached around him and slowly began to stroke his cock, Marty closed his eyes and let Quinn take him to bliss. Before he knew it, Marty felt the tingling that told him he was close, and when Quinn gripped him tighter, thrusting faster, Marty gave himself completely over to the pleasure as he came in Quinn's hand. Seconds later, he felt Quinn throb deep inside him, groaning deeply.

They both lay still for a long time, Quinn's breath tickling Marty's sweaty skin. Quinn slowly pulled out of Marty's body, and he groaned as their bodies separated. Marty waited, and he knew Quinn was removing the condom. Marty rolled over, and Quinn pulled him close, lightly kissing him on the shoulder. "Let me get the light," Quinn said, and Marty nodded, too limp and exhausted to even answer. The bed shook slightly as Quinn got up, the lights flipped off, and then Quinn joined him once again.

"I feel so special when I'm with you," Marty said into the darkness. Quinn held him close, and Marty heard a groan of assent that he took to mean that Quinn felt the same way.

"You are special," Quinn murmured, kissing him very lightly. Marty closed his eyes, quickly drifting off to sleep. The furthest thing from his mind was anything to do with his family or elections. All he thought of was Quinn, and how amazing it felt to be held in his arms, and he wondered what it would be like to be held this way every night. If only that could happen—but now that he could think again, he realized that was just as much a dream as the images in his mind when he slept.

Chapter Seven

SUNDAY morning, Quinn hated to leave Marty's bed, but he had to get up and into the bunkhouse before Marty's mother arrived. The previous day had gone well. Cassie had seen the cats, and they'd kept her and Marty's mother entertained. But watching every gesture and word had been exhausting for both of them. Quinn pushed back the covers very carefully, then slowly got up and pulled on his clothes before quietly making his way out of the room. He stopped in the living room to put on his shoes and finish with his shirt before hurrying outside and across the ranch grounds to the bunkhouse. Inside, he heard Greg moving around in his room. Without stopping, Quinn walked into his room and closed the door. In the weeks since he'd moved in here, he hadn't actually done much with the room. He'd been sleeping almost every night with Marty, and all he'd actually done in the room was change clothes. It looked it. Unpacked boxes still lined the walls, and most of the boxes, other than the ones that had some of his clothes in them, hadn't even been opened.

Quinn found fresh clothes and went down the hall to the bathroom, where he took a quick shower. Marty had told him that his mother and sister would be stopping by that morning and then would be leaving early to go home. Quinn knew from their conversations that part of his lover was so relieved by the idea he could jump for joy, but Quinn also knew that part of Marty would miss both of them when they left. Once he was done cleaning up, he dried himself and dressed before stepping out of the bathroom, nearly bumping into a still half-asleep and yawning Greg on his way in. Quinn chuckled softly as Greg scratched his butt absently through his boxers.

"Jesus, I need to wash my eyes after seeing you scratch your hairy ass," Quinn quipped. The only answer he got from Greg was a grunt as the bathroom door closed. Shaking his head, Quinn found his jacket and left the bunkhouse.

As he walked toward the main ranch house, he saw Marty's mother pulling into the drive. As soon as the car stopped, Marty's sister had her door open and then she was racing across the yard toward him. "Mr. Quinn, will you show me the tigers once more before we go home?"

Quinn took her hand and led her back toward where Marty's mother was waiting. "Wally needs to take you out there, but if you ask him nicely, I'm sure he will," Quinn answered. "Morning, Mrs. Green," Quinn said with a nod. He let go of Cassie's hand, and after touching his hat, went into the barn to get some work done, figuring it would be best to keep away from Marty until they were gone.

Things seemed to be going very well for the visit, and Quinn kept himself busy until he heard voices in the yard. Wandering out, he saw Marty's mother hugging him, and he couldn't help smiling at the relieved happiness on Marty's face. Cassie hugged Marty and then moved on to Wally, thanking him for showing her the animals. It seemed they'd made it through the entire visit without any startling revelations.

Marty's mother was getting into her car when Quinn heard an engine and saw his father's old truck turn into the drive. Quinn stepped out of the barn and watched as his father continued down the drive. Quinn locked eyes with Marty, trying to silently tell him to get his mother in her car and out of here. His father paying a visit was not a good thing, and Quinn feared that he was here to cause trouble… and most likely loud trouble.

"Call me when you get home," Quinn heard Marty say to his mother as she followed the truck with her eyes before getting in the car and closing the door. Quinn's father pulled up next to her and opened his door, getting out of the truck as Marty's mother began backing up.

"What the hell do you faggots think you're doing?" Quinn's father asked, and they all turned toward Marty's mother's retreating car for a second as it turned onto the road.

It was Wally who stepped forward, his eyes blazing. "You've been ignoring your horses and other animals, so I brought charges of animal neglect, and since the sheriff believes they have merit, all the animals at your home have been removed and brought here, where they'll be cared for. You can request a hearing to get them back, but I doubt you'll have much luck, not after what your neighbors and I saw."

"You were on my property without my permission?" Quinn saw his father step toward Wally. "You little piece of…." His dad drew back his arm, and before Quinn knew what was happening, his father went ass over teakettle and ended up sitting on his butt in the drive, shaking his head.

"I was asked to assess the health and care of your horses. The barn was filthy and there was no hay or water in any of the stalls," Wally said firmly.

"I want my property back," Quinn's father ground out between his teeth like some sort of righteously indignant teenager, and Quinn half expected him to stand up and stomp his feet.

"The horses are here by order of the sheriff, so you need to take it up with him. Now get off my ranch," Wally ordered, and Quinn saw his father flinch and back away.

"This isn't over," his father said, looking at Wally and then at Marty with such intensity that Quinn shivered.

"Yes, this is," Wally said stepping forward. "You don't get to mistreat your horses or any other animals in your care with impunity, not in this county. Now, like I said, get off my ranch before I have you removed for trespassing and press charges for willful animal endangerment, which will get you thrown in jail."

Damn. Quinn had heard stories about what Wally could be like when he was riled up, but he'd never seen it before, at least not like this. He'd also heard that Wally could take down guys much larger than himself, but to see him take down his father was pretty cool, especially when Quinn's father was acting like an ass. "I'm dead serious," Wally added when Quinn's father didn't move.

Finally, his father turned and walked back toward his truck. Quinn kept expecting his father to say something, but he got in his truck and then took off, spinning his tires as he turned out of the driveway and on to the road. "So that's your father," Marty said, and Quinn nodded, watching as his father's truck got smaller and then disappeared from view.

"Yeah, in all his adolescent glory," Quinn sighed before turning his attention back to Wally and Quinn. "How did the morning go with your mother and sister?" He really wanted to change the subject away from his father's ridiculous behavior.

"Good," Marty said. "Both my mom and sister went out to see Wally's lions and tigers. They seemed to love it. Afterwards we had breakfast and they left." Marty seemed all smiles, and as relaxed as he'd been before his mother had told him she was coming. "That was so cool the way you took down Quinn's dad," Marty said, turning to Wally. "Where'd you learn to do that?"

"I took martial arts instruction for years before I came to the ranch. At one time I thought of becoming an instructor, but I went to veterinary school instead." Wally chuckled softly. "I never thought it would come in as handy as it has out here." Wally headed inside, and both Quinn and Marty followed.

"So what's the story?" Marty asked, and Wally chuckled once again.

"When I first met Dakota, we had some problems one evening when we were out to dinner. I met Dakota when Phillip and I were out here on vacation," Wally began, sitting on the sofa. Marty remained in his chair, and Quinn sat next to him, taking Marty's hand. "The town lunk-headed bullies decided to give us grief, and you know Dakota—he's very much the alpha male. He felt he needed to protect me, but the man who decided to take me on ended up holding his nose and balls within a matter of seconds." Wally began to laugh outright. "I think it shocked Dakota and turned him on." Wally colored slightly. "Needless to say, there have been a few times when I've had to protect myself, and now no one messes with me. They don't have to like me, but they know they aren't going to get the better of me physically." Wally looked at both of them. "So what do you have planned for today?"

"I promised Jefferson that I'd finish the book we were reading," Marty said, looking at Quinn.

"I hadn't made plans. Since it's Sunday, there aren't any appointments." Quinn yawned and covered his mouth with his hand. The past few days had been exhausting.

Wally stood up and put on a jacket. "I'm going to go feed the cats and then spend the rest of the day with Dakota. I suggest you two make the most of the day as well. There's going to be plenty of work in the next few weeks. Now that spring has settled in good, everything is going to happen all at once; it always does." Wally left the room, and Quinn stood up, moving behind Marty's chair.

"I think you and I need to take Wally's advice and make the most of the quiet time we have." Quinn wheeled Marty down the hallway to his bedroom.

"I need to read to Jefferson," Marty protested lightly. Quinn opened the door to Jefferson's room and peered inside before closing the door again.

"He's still asleep," Quinn said before pushing Marty's chair into the bedroom and then closing the door.

"Quinn, you are so naughty," Marty protested, even as he transferred himself from the chair to the bed. Quinn moved the chair out of the way and was about to climb on the bed when he heard footsteps coming down the hall. He settled on the bed next to Marty and listened as Dakota and Wally talked softly. Jefferson's door opened and closed, and then Wally giggled. Quinn looked at Marty, who was about two seconds from giggling himself. Obviously, everyone in the house had had the same idea. Quinn angled his face to meet Marty's before kissing him gently. "I'm glad you had a nice visit with your mother, but I'm also glad they're gone and I get you to myself again."

Marty nodded, but his eyes remained dark, and Quinn wondered what was troubling him. Marty, however, didn't seem to want to talk about it, and instead just kissed him, hard. Quinn almost pressed Marty to tell him what was wrong, but there would be plenty of time for that. Right now, all he wanted was some quiet time with his lover, so he returned Marty's kiss with one of his own and slowly began to work Marty's clothes off his body. A distant, muted moan reached Quinn's ears and he tried to ignore it, but Marty must have heard it too, because he began to laugh, burying his head in the pillow. But very soon Marty's giggles turned to moans of his own, and they both forgot about anything outside the bedroom.

QUINN kept expecting to hear something from his father, but days turned to weeks and nothing happened. His dad's horses were still in Wally and Dakota's barn, eating hay and looking better every day. Quinn had insisted on paying for their upkeep, feeling very strongly that Wally and Dakota shouldn't incur expenses because of his family's problems.

"You look lost in thought," Marty said from behind him, and Quinn gave the chestnut horse a final stroke before turning.

"Just wondering what my dad's up to," Quinn said. "He isn't one to let a blow to his ego go unanswered, and taking something that's his definitely fits that category." The horse butted her head against him, and Quinn turned back to her, stroking her again. Marty handed Quinn a carrot, which the horse took and munched happily before looking around for more. Marty produced another carrot, and she leaned her head down to get it. "You're such a soft touch," Quinn said with a smile.

"The poor thing has had it hard," Marty explained. "Besides, I've been giving her extra treats, so I think she's come to expect them." Quinn loved Marty's smile, and over the past couple weeks, he seemed to smile more readily. Quinn had no illusions. What he had with Marty was temporary—it had to be. But it was only spring, and Marty was supposed to be there through the summer, so there was no use in worrying about it now.

"Was that your mom you were talking to earlier?" Quinn asked, knowing Marty had been on the phone when he'd left the house to work in the barn for a while.

"Yes. She filled out and returned the paperwork so I can return to school in the fall." Marty wheeled himself to one of the stalls, and the horse poked out his black head to see what Marty had for him.

"You don't sound excited about it," Quinn said, turning his attention to the horse because he didn't want Marty to see how the thought of him leaving hurt, and he knew he wasn't good at keeping it off his face.

"I am, I guess," Marty said with a sigh. "Things are so complicated now. Here, I can be myself, but as soon as I leave, I have to be what everyone expects: the former basketball player, the senator's son, the nice kid in the wheelchair. I know it seems like I'm hiding, and maybe I am. Maybe that's what I've done my entire life, I don't know." Quinn stepped closer to Marty and was about to hug him when he heard a vehicle pull into the drive and what sounded like right up to the barn. Curious, he walked to the door to see the side of his father's truck. *Speak of the devil.*

"I'm here to get my horses back," his father said.

"Call Wally," Quinn said to Marty over his shoulder.

"Who's going to take care of them for you?" Quinn asked. "You couldn't be bothered to feed them after I left." He thought about how those horses had been treated, left to stand in their own muck, with empty hay bins and water troughs. Each horse had probably lost thirty pounds by the time he and Wally had removed them, and they were so dehydrated it had taken days of careful watering to keep from overloading their delicate systems.

"I'm going to sell them," his father explained.

"What's going on?" Wally's voice rang through the barn as he strode toward them.

"Dad has come for his horses," Quinn explained, and his father shoved an official paper in front of Wally, who took it. "He says he's selling them." Wally opened the papers and remained quiet while he read them.

"Fine," Wally said, handing the papers back to his father. "I'll buy them. How much do you want?" Wally stepped closer, and Quinn's father took a step back. "Don't fuck with me. You know what happened the last time." Quinn saw his father flinch, and then he named a price that was more than they were worth. "Fine. I'll draw up the bill of sale and cut you a check." Wally walked back toward the clinic, and Quinn stared at his father.

Neither of them said anything, and after a while, his father's gaze shifted to Quinn.

"You think you're so smart and superior to everyone else." His father sneered at him.

"No, we don't," Marty said from behind him. "We're just superior to you."

Quinn bit his lower lip to keep from laughing as his father's eyes shot daggers at Marty. Wally's bootsteps rang off the concrete floor as he strode back down the aisle to where they were standing. Wally handed his father a piece of paper and waited while he signed it, and then handed him a check.

"This isn't what we agreed to," his father said indignantly.

"Check that paper from the sheriff you were waving around. It specified that the horses would be returned to you to sell once all board and feed charges had been satisfied. I deducted those charges from the check. I assume that your business is now concluded and you can get off my ranch," Wally said calmly.

"You think you know everything," his father accused. "Well, we'll see about that." Quinn's father walked back to his truck, turning it in a wide circle before bouncing down the drive.

"Doesn't take care of his truck any better than he treats his animals," Wally commented as they watched the truck bed bounce around, the shocks obviously going or gone.

"Someone's always taken care of him. His mother did until he met my mom, and once they got married, my mother took care of him. When she died, I fell into that role." Quinn wondered why he hadn't seen the complete picture before. Maybe some distance had given him perspective. "Well, at least I won't have to worry about his livestock any longer."

"Nope," Wally said, stepping to one of his purchases and rubbing her nose. "Now we know you'll be properly taken care of, and Marty can spoil you rotten with his treats." Wally walked back toward the clinic. "Let's hope that's the end of our excitement for the day." Quinn agreed wholeheartedly and followed Wally. They had appointments and they needed to get going.

Quinn made sure Wally's cases were packed, and they left, spending the rest of the morning on calls. They got back to the ranch at lunchtime. Quinn took care of their supplies, refilling the cases before heading inside. He heard Wally in the kitchen, and Marty on the phone. Quinn's heart fell to his feet when he heard the tone in Marty's voice.

"Yes, sir," he said with total resignation. Quinn poked his head into the kitchen, and Wally stopped what he was doing. "I know, Dad, but I like it here," Marty said, and Wally's expression changed to concern. He set his knife on the counter and followed Quinn into the living room.

Marty's hand shook as he held the phone, and Quinn heard the sharp tone of the person he was talking to. He assumed it was Marty's father, and he had a pretty good idea what their conversation was about.

"You'll be ready to go this afternoon," came through the phone loud and clear. Marty flinched, and his hand shook to the point Quinn thought he was about to drop the phone. Quinn sat on the sofa next to Marty and held his hand. "It's an election year and I cannot have my son providing fodder for my opponents. You know better than that, and I'm shocked you kept this from me." Quinn flinched at the way Marty's father was yelling. "The plane will be there at six o'clock. You'd better be ready and waiting when it lands." The connection went silent, and Marty stared at it for a few seconds before the phone slipped from his hand, landing on his legs before falling to the floor. Marty didn't move, and for a few seconds Quinn was afraid he wasn't breathing, but then his chest rose and Marty sighed softly, but still didn't say anything.

Quinn heard Wally get up and leave the room. A few seconds later, he heard him talking softly on the phone and then he returned. “Dakota is on his way home.”

Quinn nodded, but didn’t take his eyes off Marty. “Someone called my dad and asked him if he realized his son was staying on a ranch filled with fags.” Marty groaned. “My dad said the caller went into details of the relationships between Wally and Dakota as well as other people here.” Marty took a deep breath and closed his eyes. “My dad said just my being here was a disgrace to the family, and that if he’d known, he never would have allowed me to come here.”

“Does he know about you?” Quinn asked. “About us?”

Marty shook his head. “I don’t think so. I almost told him, but I couldn’t.”

If the anger and vitriol Quinn heard through the phone was any indication, and that was just because Marty was living at a gay-owned ranch, he couldn’t blame him for not saying anything. He probably wouldn’t, either. “It’s okay,” Quinn soothed.

“No, it’s not. I’m the biggest coward ever. I should have simply told my dad the truth and that I was staying here. But I couldn’t hurt him like that.” Marty released the brakes on his chair and wheeled himself backward, sliding his arm away from Quinn’s touch. Quinn stood up to follow him, but Wally shook his head, and Quinn sat back down.

“There’s nothing you can do,” Wally said quietly. “Marty has to make his own decision about whether he’s going to stand up for himself with his family or capitulate to what they want. We’ve all shown him the kind of relationship he can have if he’s honest and straightforward, and it’s obvious you care for him. Now he has to decide what’s important to him.”

Quinn nodded slowly. “I know, but what if he chooses them?” He swallowed hard as his chest tightened. Quinn lifted his gaze to Wally's, and he saw in Wally's expression what his head was already telling him. Marty was in his room, packing. "That's what he's already done, isn't it?"

"I'm afraid so," Wally said softly, and Quinn jumped off the sofa and walked down the hall to Marty's room. Opening the door, he saw Marty's bags lying open on the bed they'd been sharing for the past month.

"You're going to leave?" Quinn challenged. Marty didn't turn around or even answer him. "So your dad's upset. So what? You're really going to leave and go back into your little shell? After all you've seen and done here, you really think you can go back to the way you were?" Quinn swallowed hard. "Do I mean nothing to you?"

Marty stopped packing, his hands stopping in midair. Slowly, he turned his chair around. "No. You mean a great deal to me, but…." Marty went to the dresser and pulled open one of the lower drawers. "I can't make everyone happy, so I'll do what I can to hurt as few people as possible." Marty set a stack of clothes on his legs and then turned back to the bed and placed them in one of his suitcases. "You'll meet someone else and forget about me. You have to. Even if…." Marty's voice trailed off as he continued packing. "Please, Quinn, don't make this any harder than it needs to be."

Quinn heard Marty's voice break, and he stopped moving, his shoulders slumping forward. For a second, he thought Marty might turn back to him and finally tell him what he really felt, but he simply sat there, doing nothing. "Marty?" Quinn prompted.

"There's nothing else to say. This is what I have to do." Marty closed a suitcase and latched it before tugging it onto the floor with a deadening thump that matched the sound of the last bit of hope leaving Quinn's heart. Without saying anything more, Quinn turned and left the room, closing the door quietly behind him.

In the living room, he found Wally and Dakota talking quietly. The door opened and Haven strode in. "I'm heading to the west range to check on the herd," he told Dakota.

"Do you need some help?" Quinn asked. He needed to get out of here. He couldn't just sit around and wait for Marty to leave. Haven looked at Wally, who nodded.

"Be out front and ready to go in half an hour," Haven instructed. "I need to make a run home and I'll stop by on my way back. Bring a sleeping bag. We'll be back tomorrow night."

"Okay," Quinn said, and Haven left in a rush. Quinn followed him out so he could get his things together. As he walked across the yard toward the bunkhouse, Quinn refused to look back at the main house. If this was what Marty wanted, then he wasn't going to allow himself to pine away. He'd done that before and he wasn't going to do it again. Quinn knew the bravado was bullshit, but it was what kept him going, and he was determined not to shut down the way he had before. He'd been through the heartache once and come out the other side, so he could do it again.

His room looked as it had for weeks, and he rummaged through boxes until he found his sleeping bag and small tent. He also found his cooler and a waterproof bag. Shoving some warm clothes and his pillow in the bag, he got the rest of his stuff and carried it out front. Haven hadn't returned, and Quinn debated whether to go inside, but he wasn't going to be coward about this, so he climbed the stairs and went into the house. Dakota sat in the living room, not looking one bit happy. "What's happening?" Quinn asked.

"Marty's saying good-bye to Dad and then I'm driving him to the airstrip south of town. It seems his father is in such an all-fired hurry to get him away from us that he's arranged for a private plane to pick him up." The fury behind Dakota's eyes burned scorching hot, like a rangeland sunburn. Quinn heard a door close, and a few moments later Marty wheeled himself into the room. Quinn stared at Marty, debating between hugging him or slugging him in the jaw as hard as he could. Eventually he decided and leaned down, taking Marty into his arms. He didn't say anything because he knew once he began to talk he'd say things he'd regret and none of them would do a bit of good anyway.

"Take care of yourself," Quinn managed to choke out. He felt Marty return his hug, tightening his grip like he didn't want to let go. Quinn released him and straightened up. He wanted to say what was in his heart. The words were on the tip of his tongue, but he held them at bay. Quinn took a last look at Marty, memorizing the way his hair flopped to the side and the way his lips curved just so. He didn't look into his eyes, because he wanted to remember them the way they'd been when they made love. Sighing deeply, Quinn turned and walked out the door and over to Haven's truck, and after throwing his things in the back, they pulled away, with Quinn staring determinedly through the windshield.

QUINN heard the plane fly low overheard and he looked up from where he and Haven had been checking fences, the ATVs parked nearby with their gear loaded on the back. The landing gear lowered as he watched, and then the plane continued to descend until it disappeared from sight. Quinn forced himself to go back to work, his full attention glued to the posts and the barbed wire that connected them. Haven was working another section of the fence, so Quinn was largely alone. He continued working, not letting himself think about what that plane meant.

Less than an hour later, Quinn heard the plane zoom overhead as it climbed into the sky. He couldn't help following it with his eyes as it got higher and higher, moving farther and farther away, taking Marty along with it. Quinn swallowed hard, but refused to let himself think about it.

"Are you okay?" Haven asked from behind him. Quinn hadn't even heard him approach and he jumped slightly.

"I have to be. There's nothing I can do except move on and accept that he's gone." Quinn turned back to his work and tried to clear his mind of the loss that threatened to swallow him whole. "My flaw is giving my heart too easily."

Haven placed his hand on Quinn's shoulder. "That isn't a flaw. It's a gift." Quinn wasn't so sure he believed that, but didn't argue with Haven. Eventually he heard Haven walk away and he went back to the fence repairs.

They didn't stop working until right before the sun went down. Haven put up the tent while Quinn lit the camp stove and began making dinner. By the time the food was ready, the only light came from their lanterns. Quinn knew he wasn't very good company as he sat, silently eating the simple but hearty meal. Once they were done, Haven cleaned up, and Quinn unrolled his sleeping bag in the tent. It was already cold, so they'd agreed to share the tent for warmth. Quinn got ready for bed and climbed into his sleeping bag, rolling on his side so he was facing the canvas. Haven joined him a few minutes later and climbed into his own sleeping bag.

"Good night, Quinn," Haven said softly, and Quinn responded. Haven doused the light, and Quinn listened to the sounds of the night, wishing above everything that it was him and Marty in the tent. Rolling onto his stomach, he buried his head in his pillow and let go of some of what he'd been holding inside all day.

Chapter Eight

THE car pulled in front of his home, driven by one of his father's aides. Marty felt like he was in some movie, being taken for a ride to meet with the godfather. The flight in the Gulfstream his father had sent to pick him up had been agonizingly short. He'd stared out the window the entire time, hoping to catch a glimpse of the ranch as they took off. Marty thought he might have briefly seen the barn and house, but they faded fast and all Marty saw after that were mountains and valleys for the short trip to what was sure to be a less than warm reception. The car pulled to a stop, and Marty waited for the aide to bring around his chair. He offered to help, but Marty shifted himself into it on his own and wheeled himself toward the front door. The aide again offered to help, but Marty declined.

Inside, he wheeled himself over the gleaming floors to the room he'd used for those few days between coming home from the hospital and leaving for the ranch. It was the way he'd left it, with the bed in the center of the room. He was about to shift onto the bed when he heard a door open across the hall.

"You're here," his father's voice boomed, and Marty turned around to face his father's anger. They stared at one another. His father had often used the tactic in wrangling with his opponents. Marty had always backed down, but not this time—he stared right back, sitting still and silent in his chair. The longer he sat, the more his anger welled up inside him.

"I'm here as you ordered," Marty said sarcastically without looking away from his father.

"Go into my office," his father said, and Marty saw his features soften slightly. Marty hesitated before slowly propelling himself forward. Once he was through the door, his father closed it and motioned for his aides to leave. He waited until they were alone behind closed doors. "What in the hell were you thinking?" his father yelled, and Marty rolled his eyes.

"Can't you come up with anything better than that?" Marty retorted. "I liked it there. Dakota and Wally treated me with respect, and I was useful, instead of someone in a chair who had to have help with everything he did."

"Your mother and I don't think that," his father said, some of his anger dissipating.

"Is that why you kept me in the hospital for two weeks longer than I needed to be? Or was it because you didn't want the burden of helping to take care of me," Marty accused. The pain and loss of being ripped away from Quinn came bubbling to the surface. "There, no one treated me like the senator's son. I was just another one of the hands. I had my jobs to do and I did them every day."

"Did you know?" his father asked.

"Did I know what?" Marty countered.

"Did you know they were gay when you went to work for them?"

"No," Marty answered truthfully.

"But you certainly knew when your mother came for a visit," his father pressed, and Marty shrugged.

"They didn't hide anything from her. What Mom saw was how things are done at the ranch, nothing more or less," Marty answered, meeting his father's gaze. Marty knew the next set of questions his father was about to ask, he could feel it in his stomach, and his mind whirled as he tried to figure out how he was going to answer.

"But the truth remains that you kept that information from both your mother and me." Marty's father walked around to the sofa and lowered himself onto it.

"Of course I did, because I knew exactly how you'd react. I knew as soon as you found out, you'd fly off the handle and have me on a plane home so fast it would make my head spin." Marty looked around the room. "Wait… that *is* what happened."

"Don't be smart," his father snapped, acting very much the senator.

"Well, it's true." Marty said, taking a deep breath so he wouldn't say something he'd regret. "I'm here now, and you've whisked me away from that 'den of iniquity', so what's the plan?" Marty's heart beat triple time in his chest as he determined that he wasn't going to lie. If his father asked the question, he'd tell him the truth. His father didn't answer right away. "You always have a plan, so what's it going to be? What kind of dog and pony show are we going to pull out this time?" Marty watched as his father shifted on the sofa. "Let me guess. Someone came up with the bright idea of parading me out along with you and Mom so everyone could see the devoted family man whose son had a stroke." Marty could see in his father's eyes that he'd hit the nail on the head. "They figured that would counter any hint that I spent time on a ranch with gay people." Marty rolled his eyes. "Sometimes I wonder what institution for the moronic you go to for recruiting." Marty thought he saw a ghost of a smile form on his father's lips, but it faded before it could really get started.

"This election cycle is the toughest I've ever had. We haven't made any decisions yet, but yes, at some point we're going to have to make appearances as a family, and no, we will not be 'parading you out', as you put it." His father picked up some papers from the table. "Thankfully, we got you home before this whole gay thing blew up in our faces."

"Yes, thankfully," Marty said, shaking his head. "I take it we're done."

"Not by a long shot, but I have work to attend to."

Marty knew he'd been dismissed, so he glided toward the door. Before reaching for the handle, he turned around, but his father's aides were already entering the office. Marty left the office, gliding across the hall and further into the house to see if he could find his mother. She was in the kitchen working with the cook on the preparations for dinner. She turned when he entered and stepped away from what she was doing.

"You should have told me," his mother said softly, without any of the heat his father had had.

"Why? You had a nice visit and you got to know them. They're good people and you know it. If I'd have said something, you'd have treated them differently." Marty wheeled himself to the table, and his mother pulled out a chair next to his and sat down. "I don't understand what the big deal is."

"Your father is up for reelection," she said.

"Why does everything in this family revolve around Dad's reelection? We have more money than anyone in the state. Everything in this family revolves around Dad's job. When Cassie and Josh get older, are their lives going to be dominated by Dad's next reelection campaign? I sure hope not." Marty sighed. "I want to be able to live my own life, and I should be able to without the world coming to an end."

"It's just a few more months," she soothed.

"And after that I'm leaving," Marty said, what he wanted becoming more and more clear. "Maybe I'll go out east to finish college, but I'm not staying here, and I'm not going to live in his shadow any longer." Maybe he'd go back to the ranch, and if he could find a way to convince Quinn to forgive him…. "I'm tired of everything revolving around him. At the ranch, I didn't have to worry about any of that. I was responsible for me and only me." Marty lifted his gaze away from the tabletop. "I was happy there." The pain of having to leave Quinn felt very close to the surface. Marty pushed his chair back from the table and left the room without saying anything more.

He moved through the first floor to the room he'd used before. Closing the door behind him, he sat in his chair and thought. He'd never felt pain and loss like he was feeling now. The physical pain he'd endured in the hospital and therapy was nothing compared to the feeling of having his heart squeezed out of him. He'd endure a million painful therapy sessions just to make the ache in his heart go away. Closing his eyes, Marty wished….

A knock on the door pulled him out of his thoughts. He turned around and opened the door. Cassie held one of her dolls and she grinned and jumped into his lap. "I missed you," she told him, throwing her arms around his neck. At least someone was happy to see him. Marty returned her hug as tears threatened to well in his eyes. "Did you bring me pictures of the lions and tigers?"

"No, honey, but we can e-mail and ask Wally to send you some," Marty said, and she settled on his legs.

"Are you going back there?" she asked. "You look sad. Do you miss your friends?" She rested her head on Marty's chest, and he held her tight, wishing the answers to her questions were very different from the truth.

"I'm staying here with you," Marty said and forced himself to smile when he angled her head up to look at him. "My best girl," Marty added before tickling her ribs. Cassie giggled and squirmed, her playful joy music to his ears and exactly what he needed.

Josh came into the room, and Cassie climbed down. To Marty's surprise, his brother gave him a hug. "Are you home to stay?" he asked, his eyes narrowing.

"I seem to be," Marty answered. "How have things been here while I was gone?"

Josh shrugged noncommittally. "Squirt here says there were lions and tigers where you were," Josh said as he grabbed for Cassie, but she squirmed away.

"Don't call me squirt, and there were so lions and tigers. Mama saw them too." Cassie folded her arms across her chest and looked at him. Marty couldn't help grinning at his doubting brother.

"Hate to break it to you, but Wally runs a cat rescue, and there are lions and tigers, even the occasional panther." Marty yawned and tried to cover it, but he was worn out. Cassie pulled Josh out of the room, and he was left alone, but only for a few minutes until his mother came to tell him dinner was ready.

Unlike the last time he'd come home, this was no celebration. His father glared at him through most of the meal. Marty ignored him and talked a little to his mother, Cassie, and Josh, but he wasn't really in the mood for conversation. Once he was done eating, Marty pushed back from the table and rolled toward the dining room door.

"You know that no one leaves the table until everyone is done eating," his father said, and Marty stared at him for a few seconds before continuing out of the room. He'd had enough and he didn't feel like being sociable. Marty was nearly to the hallway when his chair stopped. Turning around he saw his father standing behind him.

"Go back into the dining room," his father said firmly.

"Or what? You're going to hit me? That'll look really good. 'Senator abuses son in wheelchair.' I wonder how many votes that will get you." Marty turned in the chair as best he could. "You yanked me back here because of your own narrow-minded prejudice, but I don't have to like it."

His father let go, and Marty wheeled himself toward the room he was using, slamming the door for good measure. "Damn it!" he swore once he was alone, pounding his hand on the arm of the wheelchair. An adolescent fit of temper was not going to help him. Still angry and upset, Marty transferred himself to the bed. Rummaging in the bag that hung off the back of his chair, he dug around inside, and his hand slid along the spine of a book. It was the Louis L'Amour book he'd been reading to Jefferson. Marty held it to him as he thought of everyone he'd left behind, everyone who'd been so caring and understanding. Quinn had been right—he couldn't just go back to the person he'd been before he'd come to the ranch. The genie was out of the bottle, and he couldn't put it back inside no matter how hard he tried.

It was getting dark outside and Marty closed his eyes, remembering how Quinn would help him to the sofa and then curl against him, holding him while they watched television. He missed Quinn and he wanted the dull ache in his chest to go away, but he knew it wouldn't. Marty realized, as he stared up at the ceiling, that he was in love with Quinn and had been for a while. After setting the book on the table beside the bed, Marty closed his eyes, wondering what Quinn was doing now.

"MARTY," his mother called from the doorway to his room. "You need to go to therapy." She walked inside, but he barely acknowledged her.

"Cancel the appointment and I'll go next week," he told her. Marty had no ambition to go anywhere or do anything.

"I most certainly will not. You need to get up and get ready to go." She walked into the room and dramatically pulled open the curtains. "You've moped in here for three days, and we've let you, but now it's time to get moving. You have a therapy appointment in an hour and you will be on time, so get up and wash up, because you stink, and be in the hall and ready in half an hour." She marched to the bed. "I'll do it for you if I have to and you won't like it, so move."

Marty pushed back the covers and sat up, then shifted to his chair. He left the room and made his way to the first-floor bathroom. It wasn't particularly easy, but he cleaned up and shaved before returning to his room to finish dressing. At the appointed time, he was ready to go, and his mom drove him to therapy and waited in the waiting room while one of the demons of hell guided his physical therapy. Marty went through the motions, but Hank didn't have Johnny's personality. He had the sadistic part down pat, but it wasn't tempered with humor and topped with encouragement, the way Johnny had worked. By the time they were done, Marty was already sore and ready to get the hell out of there.

"How did it go?" his mother asked once they were in the car on their way home.

"I don't like him at all," Marty said without looking at her. "He's a sadist with no personality."

His mother sighed. "And you're turning into a prickly pain in my ass. Everyone in the house knows you aren't happy, you've made that abundantly clear, but it's time you snap out of it and get on with business. If you want to walk again, then go to therapy. And if you don't, then keep complaining, and in the fall you can watch your former teammates play basketball while you sit in that chair and go nowhere." She scowled at him before turning her attention back to the road.

"Damn, Mom, you sure know how to cut through the crap," Marty said, and she smiled.

"After twenty-five years with your father, I ought to," she retorted, and Marty smiled for what felt like the first time in days. "I love your father dearly, but there are times he forgets he isn't on the Senate floor when it comes to laying the manure on thick." Marty laughed, and if she hadn't been driving, he'd have hugged her.

During the rest of the drive, they talked a lot like they had before his stroke. When they arrived at home, she helped Marty with his chair, and he glided inside to find their father waiting for them.

"It seems I haven't demonstrated the proper amount of family values," he said as Marty's mother hung up the coats. "So my campaign staff feels we need to make a very public appearance as a family. The Council for the Preservation of the American Family is holding a dinner next Thursday, and I'm scheduled to speak. We've arranged for the entire family to attend the reception and dinner. The press will be there in droves, and that should put an end to this nonsense."

"Are you sure this is necessary?" Marty's mother asked.

"I'm afraid so, dear," Marty's father told her, and then he turned his attention to Marty. "I'd appreciate it if you'd stay for the entire evening. Your mother can take Cassie and Josh home after dinner, but it would look good if you stayed."

Marty sighed. He'd known he'd be trotted out eventually, but he'd figured it would be closer to Election Day. "Sure, Dad," Marty said, swallowing down a snide comment about winning the sympathy vote.

"This is a big deal and will help set the tone for the entire campaign. The speech I'll be giving will lay out my entire campaign agenda and should put my challenger on the ropes. But in order for this to work, I need my entire family there."

Marty imagined a scene where the entire family stood—or, in his case, sat—in front of the flag while the press took pictures. "Okay," Marty said. "I'll be there for you."

His father stepped closer, placing his hand on Marty's shoulder. "I knew I could count on you," his father said with a smile, and Marty nodded as his father returned to his office. Marty looked at his mother, who seemed resigned to whatever she had to do. His legs hurt from therapy, so he went to his room to lie down for a while. At the ranch, he'd have read to Jefferson for a while, but here he really didn't have anything he needed to do. Marty thought of calling Quinn to see how he was doing, but he wasn't sure his call would be welcome, so instead he transferred himself to the bed and closed his eyes.

As soon as he did, Quinn's face flashed in his mind, his smile making Marty smile. Quinn moved closer, and Marty was instantly hard, throbbing in his pants. He kept his eyes closed, knowing as soon as he opened them his imaginary Quinn would be gone, and that was all he had now.

Marty imagined Quinn stripping for him—there was even music in the background. Quinn's shirt hit the floor, followed by the thunk of his shoes. His pants were next, and then Marty's imaginary Quinn stood right next to him in nothing but black briefs and a smile. Marty reached for himself, his hand sliding into his pants.

A knock on the door instantly scratched away his fantasy, and Marty yanked his hand away from himself, adjusting things so he wouldn't completely embarrass himself. "Yes," he said with a hitch in his voice.

The door opened and his father walked in. "I've been working on my speech, and I was wondering if you'd listen to it." His father sat on the edge of the bed.

"What about the minions?" Marty asked with a smile, and his father laughed.

"They helped me write it, and I need to make sure it conveys what I want to say," his father explained, and Marty sat up, getting himself comfortable. "I'll start with an appropriate introduction and then get to the heart of the speech." Marty rested back on some pillows and listened.

"The American family is under threat. No longer are couples staying together until death do us part. We have divorce, children out of wedlock, and, of course, the thrusting of gay marriage down the throat of the God-fearing American public." His father paused, and Marty felt his breath hitch as he tried to school his expression. "The institution of marriage is a sacred bond between one man and one woman. It is the basis upon which our families are founded. Yet this most basic unit of our society is under threat, and that threat must be countered, and that must start now." Marty's father stood up and began pacing the room. "We can no longer sit by as court after liberal court strips away the most fundamental building blocks of this country." His dad was really on a roll, and Marty felt as though his throat was about to seize up. "And that is why I am proposing and championing a constitutional amendment to define marriage in this country as the union of a man and a woman. Applause, applause," his father added. "I understand this amendment has little chance of passage, but it will send a very powerful message that we will not stand for these continuing attacks on our most fundamental societal building block." His father paused before turning to look at him. "From here, I'll go into my other policy items. What do you think? Is it powerful?"

Marty was sure his eyes were as wide as saucers. "It's powerful," was all Marty could say. His father seemed pleased with that response and walked toward the door. "I'll see you later." Marty saw his father nod as he left the room, making notes on his page as he walked. "Dad, do you think you could send in one of your aides to help get me up the stairs?" He desperately needed a shower and he needed one now.

"Sure." His father continued to his office, and Marty got together his kit and comfortable clothes. Levi, a huge hulk of a man who was also surprisingly intelligent, came into the room. Marty set his things on his legs and Levi carefully lifted him out of the chair and carried him through the house and up the stairs like he weighed next to nothing. Levi set Marty on a seat in the tub, and Marty thanked him for the help.

"Call me when you're dressed and I'll take you back down." Levi left the room and closed the door behind him. Marty undressed carefully and set out everything he needed before pulling the curtain and turning on the water. He'd hoped the hot water would wash away the uneasy feelings he'd had as he listened to his father's vitriolic speech, but it couldn't—nothing could. He wondered what his father would say if he knew that his own son was one of the people he was railing against. Scrubbing his body hard, Marty wished he could scrub away that part of himself. Then his hand stopped in mid-movement. At the ranch, he'd been happy with who he was. Quinn had cared for him and accepted him for who he was. Everyone had. He hadn't needed to feel ashamed or embarrassed. Hell, Quinn had slept in his room almost every night and no one had said anything. Marty finished washing, and after rinsing himself well, he turned off the water and carefully reached for a towel. After drying off, he dressed carefully and then used his cell phone to call for Levi, who gently carried him back downstairs to his room, setting him on the bed.

"Thank you," Marty said, and Levi smiled before returning to his father's office. Marty turned on the television. He felt as trapped and helpless as he'd ever felt in his life. His own father sounded like he was going to war and the enemy was him. He knew what he wanted to do, but he was scared. At least he could admit that, but what was he going to do about it? He had no idea.

THE following Monday afternoon, Marty's father summoned him to his office. After knocking, Marty pushed open the door. His mother sat on the sofa with Levi beside her, a folder open, resting on his lap. "Excellent. Marty, we wanted to take a few minutes to go over what we expect to happen on Thursday," his father said, coming around from behind his desk.

"The cocktail hour will be informal," Levi began. "I've already called ahead and made sure there will be soda and fruit drinks for the children. I was informed that the cocktail hour was actually a meet and mingle and that no alcohol will be served in deference to the many religious groups that support the foundation. They want the reception and dinner to be for families and are encouraging attendees to bring their children. They have to pay for them, of course." Levi shifted slightly as he quickly reviewed his notes. "I was also assured that there will be child care available during the program portion of the evening." Marty glanced at his mother and saw the "no way in hell" look in her eyes.

"Mrs. Green will take the children home after dinner. Arrange for a limousine to be available to take them home," the senator said, and Levi made a note before continuing.

"During the reception, they've asked if you'd make yourself available for photographs, with the proceeds to go to their political action funds, and after dinner they're asking if your entire family could stand on stage for photographs and a brief question-and-answer period." Levi paused before shifting on the sofa to face Marty. "We'd very much like it if at the appropriate time you would introduce your father for his speech. A sincere introduction coming from you in your own words would be quite powerful and could be the sound bite for the news." Levi shifted his portfolio and handed Marty a sheet. "We took the liberty of drafting something for you."

Marty glanced at the paper, an introduction in his own words—written by one of his father's political aides. That was going to be touching. Marty reminded himself that politics was theater and nothing more. "I'll rework this into my own words," Marty said, and Levi looked at the senator. Marty saw a concerned expression flash across his father's face. "If you want the introduction in my own words, then that's what you'll get. If you want your words, I'll take this page with me and read it out loud. The choice is yours."

"Just use that as a guide. Your own words will be more powerful," his father agreed, and Levi nodded before continuing.

"Dinner will be served, and there's a table reserved for the family. Two seats have been reserved at that table. The proceeds from those chairs will also benefit their political action fund. I understand each seat sold for ten thousand dollars. After the meal, the head of the organization will speak briefly. He'll introduce Marty, who will in turn introduce you. After your speech, they've asked if you could remain available for half an hour for additional pictures and questions." Levi concluded his rundown for the evening and waited for additional comments or items.

"Seems like the usual political evening," the senator said. Marty nodded absently as he read the introduction that had been written for him. There was no way he could say this crap; the words would get caught in his throat. Six months earlier, he could have read the page without a problem, but now he couldn't say that he, like his father, believed in the power of the traditional family, like they'd written for him. Marty was already reworking the speech in his mind, removing the crap and going for simple honesty, when his phone rang.

Marty pulled it out of his pocket and saw Dakota's phone number. Backing away from the gathering, he moved to one of the corners. "Hello," he said softly, and he saw all eyes on him. Marty stared back, and they had the decency to look away even if he knew they were all still listening.

"Marty, it's Wally." Marty knew something was very wrong. He hoped Quinn was okay. "Jefferson had a massive stroke early this morning. He was rushed to the hospital." Wally sniffled, and his voice broke. "Dakota made the decision not to put him on life support, and he died half an hour ago. It was peaceful and he wasn't in any pain. After the stroke, he never regained consciousness." Marty turned toward the wall, not wanting the others in the room to see the tears forming in his eyes. "Of course we haven't made funeral arrangements yet, but we'd all very much like you to be here if you can."

"I'll do my best, I promise," Marty said, sniffing. "Thank you for letting me know."

"Of course. I'll call you when I know more," Wally said, and then he ended the call.

Marty placed the phone back in his pocket, but didn't move. "What is it?" his mother asked from behind him, and Marty wiped his eyes before turning around.

"Jefferson passed away," he told his mother. "He had a stroke early this morning. Wally said it was peaceful and painless."

"Does he know when the funeral is?" she asked, and Marty shook his head. "Let me know, and I'll arrange to send flowers for you."

Marty nodded. "Yes. I mean no." Something welled inside Marty, loss building on the heartache that had been gnawing at him ever since he'd arrived here. "I'm not sending flowers."

"If that's what you want," his mother agreed, and she turned back to where his father and Levi were talking.

"I'm going to the funeral," Marty announced, and all conversation stopped as heads turned in his direction. Marty stared at Levi and tilted his head sharply toward the door. Levi didn't look at the senator before he closed his folder and stood up, then walked briskly toward the exit. Marty waited until the door closed before speaking. "I'm going to Jefferson's funeral," Marty reiterated.

"No, you're not," his father countered.

"Yes, I am," Marty countered firmly.

"I need you at the dinner on Thursday. Like your mother said, you can send flowers and a card."

Marty scoffed as his courage continued to build. "I'm not going to any dinner for the Council to Promote Discrimination, Bigotry, Hatred, and Hypocrisy." Marty balled the piece of paper he still held in his hand. "I'm gay, Dad," he yelled, throwing the balled paper at his father. He'd finally had the courage to say those two words to his father. Both his parents stared at him with open mouths. "I've known I was gay for a long time, but it wasn't until I spent time at the ranch that I was able to come to terms with who I am."

"They did this to you," his father accused weakly, and Marty saw his mother begin to cry.

"No one did anything to me except help me accept who I've been for a long time," Marty said as calmly as he could while his heart raced a mile a minute. Slowly, he moved closer to both of them. "This isn't something I've chosen, but a part of myself I've known about, but refused to acknowledge, for a long time. I know this is hard for you to accept, and you'll need some time, but I can't hide who I am any longer." Marty turned to his father. "I couldn't let you continue to attack me and people like me without knowing who it was you were hurting." Marty turned to his mother and took her hand, half expecting her to pull it away. "I know this hurts, but I couldn't keep who I was from you any longer. I've been hiding and hurting for so long."

"But," she began with tears running down her face. "Are you sure? You're so young. How can you know?" She dabbed her eyes with a tissue from the box on the table.

"Yes, Mom, I'm sure. I didn't just decide I was gay. The only thing I decided was to tell you, and it's the hardest thing I've ever done in my life. I know you're disappointed, afraid, and wondering about so many things, but I want you to know that you didn't do anything wrong. I just know that I was born this way, and this doesn't change the way I feel about you." Marty couldn't stand to see his mother cry. That hurt almost as much as the ache that had filled his heart since he'd left Quinn.

"This can't be happening," his father said softly. "How can this happen now?"

Marty moved away from his mother. "Is that all you care about? Your reelection? I'm your son and I just told you that I'm gay, and all I hear is how could I do this to you and how is it going to affect my campaign? Well, fuck you, Dad!" Marty wheeled himself toward the door. "I'm going to Jefferson's funeral, and you can make any excuses you want to the Council for Peddling Crap, but I'm going to the funeral of the man I wish was my father." Marty yanked open the office door and raced across the hall to the room he was using, then slammed the door closed.

Marty took deep breaths to settle down. He half expected his father to come charging after him, but Marty heard no footsteps in the hall. "You handled that really well," Marty said out loud. He probably could deal with his dad following him and yelling. Then at least he'd know his dad was dealing with it in his own way, but the silence was worrying him. He also had to figure out how he was going to travel the hundreds of miles from Cheyenne to Wally and Dakota's ranch. He still couldn't drive, and it was highly unlikely his parents would arrange transportation. Marty tugged his phone out of his pocket and looked through his contact list, wondering who he could call for help. One name stood out as a possibility, and Marty dialed the number, hoping he was right.

"Hello," a tentative voice said.

"Pat, it's Marty Green," he said as cheerfully as he could, but he heard nothing from the other end of the line.

"Are you calling to give me grief too?" Pat asked, which took Marty aback.

"About what?" Marty asked.

"I guess the rumor mill hasn't reached you yet. I'm surprised. It got around campus in record time. I came out to my folks and some of the guys on the team, and it spread like wildfire," Pat said, and Marty knew he'd been right and he breathed a small sigh of relief.

"I hadn't heard, but I can't say I'm surprised. There were a few hushed things said earlier in the year, but I didn't pay them any mind."

"Then why did you call?" Pat asked guardedly, and Marty chuckled before telling Pat about the conversation he'd had with his parents. "No shit!" Pat said. "I never would have guessed." The laughter died rather quickly. "How are they taking it?"

"Don't know. I left the room and they haven't come out yet," Marty said, listening for any signs of movement, but hearing nothing. "I don't know if that's a good sign or not. How about you?"

"I think my folks would like me to simply disappear," Pat said. "They haven't yelled or anything, but they haven't talked about it either." Pat sighed. "Sorry, you called for something, and I doubt it was to share war stories."

"Well, I called because I didn't know who else to call, and I was hoping you might understand what I wanted to ask. It looks like maybe I was right. I need a ride to a funeral out near Jackson," Marty explained, telling Pat about Wally, Dakota, and the rest of the guys at the ranch. His voice broke when he tried to tell Pat about Jefferson, so he let it go for now. There would be plenty of time during the drive to explain about Dakota's amazing dad.

"Are you kidding me? Does this place really exist? It sounds like the promised land," Pat said excitedly.

"Yes, it's real," Marty said.

"Then when do you want to leave?"

MARTY had finished making arrangements with Pat a while ago, and they were going to leave in the morning. He still hadn't heard anything from his parents, so he poked his head out of the room. The door to his father's office was closed. Figuring he'd face the music now rather than later, he rolled up to it and knocked softly. A few seconds later, it opened, and his father stood looking down at him. Without a word, he opened the door further and Marty glided inside.

His mother still looked a bit shocked, but more composed than she'd been when he left. But she looked at his father, and Marty knew whatever was coming would be from him. "We don't understand this at all," his father began.

"Of course you don't," Marty agreed. "It took me a long time and a great deal of soul searching to figure it out myself." Marty saw from his father's expression that he hadn't been expecting that response.

"Your mother and I have talked a great deal over the past few hours, about many things. I suggested we check you into a facility that can cure you, and she about took my head off."

"No child of mine is going to be handed over to quacks," she said with fire in her eyes.

Marty smiled at her. *Yay, Mom.*

"There is one undeniable fact that both of us agree on: we still love you. But this puts us… me… in a difficult position."

"I know. Why do you think I didn't tell you about any of it? I've been struggling with this for a long time. I wanted to tell both of you, but didn't feel I could." Marty took a deep breath. "You always said not to embarrass the family and to avoid the appearance of impropriety. I knew how to avoid it in my behavior, and I have, but what if it was part of me?" Marty couldn't look at his father any longer. "What if you didn't choose me?"

"What disappoints me most is that you'll never have children," his mother told him.

"I could adopt or find a surrogate once I have a partner." Marty turned to his dad. "I know this isn't the right time, but we need to talk. This whole amendment thing is wrong. Let's say I do adopt a child with my partner, and you and Mom are gone. What will happen to him if something happens to me? The state, foster care—that isn't an issue if we're married. This whole marriage battle is useless, Dad, because you've already lost. In ten years, this whole antigay family-values thing will be a dead issue. Young people don't care if you're gay or not. Gay marriage is going to happen. You can't stop it. The only thing you're doing is trying to impress your prejudices and preconceived notions on the next generation. Young people are in favor of gay marriage by a wide margin, so let the whole thing die. It didn't have a chance of passage anyway. Use your authority and presence to win this election on what you've always stood for: personal freedom."

"It isn't that simple," his father said.

"Actually, it is. You've never pandered to the lowest common denominator before, and that's what's made me most proud to have you as my dad. I've seen the other idiots in Congress on television and was always proud that you were better and smarter than that. They'll say anything today for a vote and regret it tomorrow. You never did that, so why are you doing it now?" Marty looked out the large windows that looked over their front lawn. "They want black and white, but it's harder when the shades of gray are right in the room with you."

His father stared at him for a long while. "You would have made a great politician. Well, all except the part about calling my colleagues idiots. That may be true, but we can't say that." His father's slight smile faded. "That doesn't change the fact that you've dropped quite a bombshell on us today."

Marty nodded. "No, it doesn't. I'll answer the questions I can, but remember this. I'm still the same person you raised. The only difference is that the person I'll fall in love with will be another man instead of a woman."

"I wish I could understand all of this," his mother said.

"You will. It takes time," Marty said. "I've just had a head start."

She nodded, still looking a little like her eyes were rolling. "Is there someone…?"

Marty wasn't prepared to talk about Quinn right now. "There might be, I don't know," Marty answered honestly. "I'll find out tomorrow, I guess, when I get back there."

"How are you going to get there?"

"One of the guys from the team is going to take me," Marty explained before hugging his mother tight. "I know this is hard for both of you, and I'm grateful you're willing to try."

"Of course we are," his mother told him as she began to cry again. "You're my boy."

His father seemed more tentative, but he gripped Marty's shoulder. "I don't understand any of this, but you're still my son, no matter what." Marty placed his hand on his dad's. "How long will you be gone?"

"Probably until school starts in the fall. That is, if I still have a job," Marty said. Then he moved backward, away from his parents. "I have to do this, but you're both welcome to visit, you know that. But I need to be on my own for a while. I know you both love me, and I can't tell you how grateful I am for your support." Marty felt tears forming in his eyes. "I know this is hard for both of you, and you have a million questions, which I'll try to answer as best I can." Marty waited to see if any of those questions surfaced, but it seemed they'd all talked enough for now, so Marty moved toward the door.

"Marty," his dad called, and he stopped. "Do you really wish someone else was your dad?"

Marty had never heard that kind of hurt in his father's voice before, and it tore at him. He'd done that with a careless remark that had hit home. Moving back to his father, Marty wheeled right up to him and wrapped his arms around his waist. "No, Dad," he said softly as his father's hands rested on his hair. His father breathed raggedly, and Marty realized just how hard he was working to hold himself together. "I love you, Dad," Marty said before releasing him and backing away. "I love you both," Marty said as his own voice broke.

He opened the office door and left the room, breathing a huge sigh of relief. All those weeks of worry and fear were for nothing. Yes, telling his parents he was gay had been painful, and he had put his father in a difficult position, but it wasn't as though he planned to shout his sexuality from the rooftops. He was about to go into his room when he heard footsteps. Cassie and Josh walked toward him, Cassie carrying a book, and Josh with a worried look on his face.

"You're leaving again, aren't you?" Josh challenged, and Cassie's smile fell from her face.

"I'm going back to work, yes. A special friend died, and I need to go to his funeral, and then, hopefully, I'll be staying to work." Marty patted his knees, and Cassie climbed onto his lap. "But both of you can come visit."

"Can I feed the lions?" Cassie asked. She was definitely the fearless one in the family.

"You'll have to ask Wally when you visit," Marty said as he wheeled toward the bedroom. Cassie scrambled onto the bed, and Marty settled next to her. After opening her book, he began to read. Josh left the room and returned a while later with his video game console, and the three of them took turns playing.

At dinnertime, they ate as a family. The conversation was a bit strained, but at least there was no yelling. Once the meal was over, Marty called Wally and filled him in on the details of his plans, including Pat giving him a ride. "He's welcome to stay," Wally said right away. "Do you want me to tell Quinn you're coming?"

"No. I'll call him," Marty answered, but when he tried Quinn's phone, all he got was voice mail. Marty left a brief message asking Quinn to call him, but no return call came.

QUINN listened to Marty's message about coming for Jefferson's funeral, but then he deleted it and tossed his phone on his bed in the bunkhouse. His heart had ached every minute of every day since Marty had left, and now he was coming back for a few days to attend Jefferson's funeral. Big deal. If it wasn't for everything Wally, Dakota, and Jefferson had done for him, Quinn would take off into the mountains and camp for a few days until all this was over. But Jefferson had meant a great deal to him, so Quinn figured he could suck it up for a few days, and just stay out of Marty's way until he left again. He went to clean up and then climbed into bed, wishing, the way he had every night, that things could be different.

Chapter Nine

QUINN kept himself as busy as possible. He knew that Marty and his “friend” were driving over for the funeral and that they were expected to arrive at any time. He’d already cleaned and sanitized every surface in the clinic at least twice, and he kept praying for a call so he could go out with Wally and then wouldn’t have to be here when Marty arrived.

Once there was nothing more to do in the clinic, Quinn worked in the barn before deciding it was time to take a ride and saddling one of his horses. He needed some fresh air, sunshine, and space so he could breathe and clear his head.

Getting his supplies from the tack room, he brushed down Largo and got him saddled before putting on his coat and then led the chestnut gelding out of the barn. As he reached the barn door, he saw a strange car pull into the drive, and Quinn realized he hadn’t been quick enough. He thought about pretending he hadn’t seen them, jumping on the horse, and heading out as fast as he could without looking like he was running. But he couldn’t do that. Instead, he held the reins and waited for the car to pull to a stop.

A guy about Marty’s age got out and pulled out a wheelchair, then rolled it around to the passenger door. Quinn felt like a fool just standing there, so he led Largo back to his stall and figured he might as well get this over with.

“Quinn,” Marty called with a huge smile on his face. “This is Pat. He and I played basketball together.”

"It's nice to meet you," Pat said shaking his hand. "Marty has been talking about you nonstop for the last three hundred miles, so it's good to put a face with the name."

"He has?" Quinn asked, returning Pat's handshake, then looking at Marty, who grinned up at him from his chair. Quinn narrowed his eyes slightly and was about to ask what was going on when he saw Dakota come out of the house. The big cowboy walked over to Marty and hugged him tight, practically lifting him out of the chair. Neither said anything, and Quinn saw the grief plain on Dakota's face.

"He wasn't in pain," Dakota said softly about his father, but it was plain Dakota was feeling a great deal of it. The dark marks beneath Dakota's eyes were even more pronounced than they'd been the day before. Marty reached into the bag that hung on his chair and pulled out a book.

"I accidentally took this with me when I left. I was reading it to Jefferson and forgot it was in the bag." Marty handed the book to Dakota, who took it, and after holding it for a few seconds, he passed it back to Marty.

"Please keep it. You made him happy," Dakota said before turning to Pat. "Dakota Holden," he said, extending his hand. "You must be Pat, and I'm sorry we aren't meeting under happier circumstances." Dakota released Pat's hand. "I can show you to your room if you like." Pat opened the trunk and pulled out a suitcase before following Dakota toward the house.

"How long are you staying?" Quinn asked, shifting slightly from foot to foot.

"Wally said I still have a job if I want it, so I'll be here until classes start in the fall."

"What about the senator?" Quinn asked skeptically.

"I told my folks I was gay, and while they weren't thrilled, they're trying to understand." Marty's gaze met his. "There wasn't a day I didn't miss you until it hurt. I know this is a hard time to come back, but when Wally told me about Jefferson, all I could think about was you and how I'd messed things up by leaving and taking the coward's way out. Jefferson told me once that you only get one life and he didn't regret anything in his, so he was happy. I kept hearing those words after I talked with Wally, and I realized the only place I could be happy was here with you. Can you forgive me?"

Quinn didn't move and didn't know what to say. He was being given exactly what he'd wanted since the day Marty had left. "Of course I can, but what about the end of the summer, when you leave again? We're going to be right back where we were, and I don't think I can go through this again."

Marty reached out and took his hand. "We'll figure it out together."

"But," Quinn began, and Marty tugged slightly on his hand.

"I love you, Quinn," Marty said, and Quinn's throat went dry. "I know it's stupid, but as soon as that plane took off, I realized what I felt and that I'd never told you. I'm sorry it took so long for me to put words to what I was feeling, and even longer to actually say it." Marty looked so earnest, and as Quinn looked into his huge eyes, he felt his heart melt and then leap for joy.

Quinn knelt on the ground in front of Marty's chair, hugging him close. "I missed you too. I wasn't worth a crap the entire time you were gone." Quinn looked deep into Marty's eyes and lightly stroked his cheek. "I love you too, but if you leave me again the way you did, I'll follow you and hunt you down like a dog, and bring you back to a house without ramps." Quinn smiled. He couldn't resist the last part. "I'm not going through that kind of heartache again."

Marty chuckled as he tugged Quinn closer. "A house without ramps? Then I'd better get busy learning to walk again."

"Only if you promise not to go anywhere," Quinn said seriously.

"I won't, not without you," Marty told him, and Quinn brought their lips together in a gentle kiss that held a massive amount of promise.

"Okay, now that we've got that settled, we should probably get inside and comfort our friends. They've had a very tough time of things for the last couple of days." Now that the ache that had threatened to overwhelm him for weeks had been soothed, Quinn's concern shifted to Wally and Dakota. Both men had been grieving deeply. Marty nodded, and the happy expression faded from his face with a soft sigh.

Quinn helped Marty get his things, and they moved inside. Pat was sitting on the sofa looking a bit lost, while Dakota and Wally sat quietly in their chairs, staring blankly at one another. "Is Marty in the same room?" Quinn asked, and once Wally nodded, he placed Marty's things in his room before joining the others.

"Jefferson would hate this," Marty said after everyone sat for a while, wondering what they should say. "He wasn't gloomy or unhappy even during the last weeks I was here. He knew and he was ready." Marty looked to Dakota. "He told me once that he'd seen all the things he most wanted in his life come true: you finishing medical school and building a happy and contented life with Wally here on your family's land."

"He said that to you?" Dakota asked.

"Yes. He was trying to help me understand what was truly important, but I didn't realize that at the time. Thankfully, I do now." Marty choked up, and Quinn reached for his hand. He noticed Pat watching them and then looking away.

"We're having a memorial service on Thursday. Dad and I opted for cremation and a simple service."

"And afterwards?" Marty asked, but Dakota shrugged and shook his head. He obviously hadn't thought that far. The front door opened, and Haven walked in with Phillip, Wilson, and Steven behind him. Everyone looked dour. Jefferson had touched all their lives in some way.

"Marty was just asking about the plans after Jefferson's memorial," Quinn explained once introductions had been made and everyone had sat down.

"Do you mind if we plan a wake?" Marty asked.

"You mean have a party?" Dakota asked without any energy.

"Yeah," Haven said, perking up and sitting forward in his chair. "Your dad loved the summer cookouts and he loved a good party." Haven stood up and walked over to Dakota. "Your father was in many ways a dad to almost everyone in this room at some point. He had personality and a heart that was bigger than life. Why not send him off with a bang instead of a whimper?" Quinn looked around the room, and everyone nodded slowly, and eventually Dakota did as well. "Good. Phillip and I will take charge of the planning."

"I can help too," Pat said quietly from his end of the sofa.

"Thanks, all of you," Dakota said as he stood up and quietly left the room, with Wally trailing behind him. Marty watched him go and then looked at Quinn.

"Wally said he hasn't slept much in days," Quinn explained, hoping he was going to lie down for a while. The group spent the next hour making plans, and then they split up to make their phone calls and get everything in motion.

"DID you get everything done?" Marty asked as Quinn joined him in bed that night.

"Yes. Did you?"

Marty nodded his answer as he rolled onto his side, curling close to Quinn. “Thank you for taking Pat riding this evening. He said the two of you talked quite a bit.”

“We did,” Quinn said, silencing Marty with a kiss. “I don’t want to talk about anything other than you.” Quinn pressed Marty onto the mattress, climbing on top of him. “I know what’s happening outside this room and what the next few days are going to be like. But right here in this room, it’s just you and me.” Quinn stroked slowly up Marty’s side. “I need to make sure you’re really back.”

“I’m back and I’m not going anywhere,” Marty said, and Quinn kicked off the covers as he licked the base of Marty’s shoulder, eliciting a sigh that quickly turned to a deep throaty groan. “I lay awake nights, eyes closed, thinking of you.”

Quinn smiled against Marty’s skin. “Did you stroke yourself thinking of me?” Quinn asked before lightly sucking one of Marty’s sensitive nipples. “You did, didn’t you?” Quinn kept licking and sucking and didn’t stop until Marty muttered a yes. “Show me,” Quinn muttered, sliding off Marty’s body. “Show me what you did to yourself. I’m right here and I want to see how much you missed me.”

“Quinn,” Marty whined softly. “I don’t need that now. I have you.”

Quinn nuzzled Marty’s neck again, licking and sucking lightly on his skin. He didn’t want to mark him because attending a funeral with a hickey was simply tacky. “Show me, Marty,” Quinn whispered, running a finger around the nipple closest to him. “I want to see, and I’ll definitely make it worth your while. Show me how just thinking of me would get you hot.”

Marty began lightly stroking along his length, and Quinn watched every movement, smiling as he kissed Marty hard. “I do love you,” Quinn said, and he felt Marty shift his arms until they were around him, pulling him closer.

"I love you too," Marty responded, the words muffled against his lips, but Quinn didn't care. He had Marty in his arms and that was where he belonged. This was where they belonged—together. "Make me yours again."

Quinn groaned deep in his throat as he reached over to the nightstand. He pulled open the drawer and found the bottle of lube. After slicking his fingers, he waited for Marty to roll over before sliding them between his perfectly round, firm butt cheeks. Slowly and carefully, he prepared his lover, listening to the sounds of need that filled the room. Marty squirmed and moaned as one finger became two. After he could take no more of Marty's love noises, Quinn rolled on a condom, lubed it, and then helped Marty roll onto his side. After lying down next to him, pulling Marty close, Quinn slowly pressed into his lover's body.

Marty's heat surrounded him, and Quinn had to calm himself to keep from driving into Marty's body. He'd missed his lover so damned much, and his body remembered and wanted what he'd been missing while Marty was gone. Quinn thought unsexy thoughts for a few seconds until his hips rested against Marty's butt. Stroking his chest, Quinn waited as his cock throbbed and jumped inside Marty's tight passage. He waited until Marty moved before slowly withdrawing. He loved the feel of Marty's skin against his, and he kept his movements small, so as not to break the contact between them.

"Is this okay?" Quinn whispered into Marty's ear, getting a slow groan in response. Taking that as a yes, he stroked down Marty's belly before wrapping his fingers around Marty's cock, stroking his lover in time to his slow thrusts.

"Jesus, Quinn, you're going to kill me," Marty whispered breathily.

"No, I'm just loving you, and I want to take my time," Quinn whispered into Marty's ear, licking the skin lightly, and

Marty whimpered. "I want to spend the next, say, thirty or forty years loving you."

"Yes," Marty answered, and Quinn snapped his hips as they moved together. He held off as long as he could, driving Marty as wild as possible along the way. Within a matter of minutes, Marty was making a steady stream of small noises that joined with Quinn's, filling the room with the sounds of their love.

Quinn heard Marty's breathing become ragged and felt him snap his hips into his hand. Marty's groans intensified and then he cried out, his entire body stiffening as he came over Quinn's hand. The feel of Marty's body around him and knowing the pleasure he'd just given his lover sent Quinn over the edge in a mind-numbing, skin-tingling climax.

After holding Marty for a long time, their bodies separated on their own, and Quinn slipped off the bed, locating a small towel Marty kept in the nightstand. After a quick cleanup, he turned out the dim light and climbed back in bed. Quinn held Marty tight, the warmth of his lover keeping the sadness that lurked outside the door at bay for the night.

THE sun shone gloriously after the raging storm the evening before. Lightning had flashed and thunder had rattled the windows and shaken the earth, like nature herself was upset at Jefferson's passing. Now the sky was a brilliant blue, the air warm with a steady breeze—in a word, perfect. Half the town had shown up for Jefferson's memorial service, which Dakota had insisted on holding at this particular spot in the range just west of the barn. A table had been set up, covered with a white cloth that fluttered slightly in the gentle wind, and half a dozen arrangements of stunning red roses surrounded the bronze urn that contained Jefferson's ashes. Quinn had helped the guys set up chairs, but the turnout had been so large that the ladies had been given the chairs and most of the men stood around the edges, hats of all sorts in their hands. After the storm, Quinn had been afraid that the land would be too wet for the service, but it had dried in the breeze and sun.

"I want to thank you all for coming to say good-bye to a man who touched everyone he met," the minister began, lifting his voice to heaven. "Jefferson Holden never talked about what was right and good; he lived it every day of his life." Quinn didn't have to look around him to know people were nodding in agreement because he saw Marty sitting in his chair, nodding right along with him. "He never turned away a person in need, and somehow, even in his later years, when he was largely confined to his bed, he managed to still bring life and joy to all our lives." Quinn swallowed and wiped a tear from his eyes as the minister continued. "Jefferson gave me a bit of advice a number of years ago, during my first week as minister here. He said to keep the sermons short, interesting, and to preach about the good instead of railing on the bad. So today I'm going to do all those things. While we all mourn the loss of a dear friend and father, we also celebrate a life lived the absolute fullest possible every single day." The minister stepped forward and said a soft prayer before stepping aside.

A few moments later, a single guitar began to play from the center of the gathering. Wilson's deep rich voice surrounded the gathering before being carried out on the breeze as he sang a simple version of "Amazing Grace." Tears flowed down Quinn's cheeks, and he felt Marty take his hand, holding it tight as the music swelled, built, and then floated away.

Dakota said a few words about his father and invited others to do the same. Time had no meaning as the group cried, sniffled, chuckled, and smiled as impressions of Jefferson's life were shared.

"Thank you all," Dakota said as he stood in front of the table once again. "My father specifically requested that his service be held out here. He wanted his final farewell to be held on the land he loved so much." Dakota lifted the urn off the table, and Quinn felt Marty squeeze his hand before letting go. He stared in amazement as Marty slowly stood up. Quinn heard the others behind them standing up as well. Carefully, Quinn took hold of Marty's arm to steady him, and watched as Marty put one foot in front and took a small step away from his chair and toward his future—and maybe their future. Quinn placed an arm around Marty's shoulder, supporting him the way he would for the rest of his life if Marty allowed him.

Together they watched as Dakota stepped away from the group and walked out onto the range. "Dad," Dakota said as he opened the lid on the urn. "We love you, Dad. Be happy and free." The breeze picked up, and Dakota tossed the ashes into the air. They were immediately picked up by the wind and carried away, scattered over the land that Jefferson loved so much.

Everyone was quiet for a while, and then the gathering broke up. People talked as they helped carry the chairs and table back toward the house. Quinn and Pat helped Marty sit back down and pushed his chair carefully across the uneven ground. As they approached the yard, Quinn heard the band start to play, and Willie Meadows began to sing.

They approached a small group standing off to the side. Dakota, Wally, Haven, and Phillip stood apart, listening and watching as the party got started. "Jefferson would have loved this," Wally said, and Dakota nodded his agreement before stepping away to join the others. Phillip grabbed Pat's hand, tugging him along as he and Haven joined the party as well.

"A funeral has to be the strangest way for two people to realize what they really wanted," Marty said, shaking his head.

"I prefer to think of it as Jefferson's last gift," Quinn said before smiling at Marty, and then they too joined the party.

Epilogue

MARTY stood on the edge of the basketball court, nervously looking around as he waited for the game to start. The last time he'd actually played in a game was when he'd had his stroke, a little more than two years earlier. He'd fought hard to come back, enduring a year of additional physical therapy until, at the beginning of his junior year, he was allowed to practice on a limited basis with the basketball team. They'd placed him on the team for the year, and tonight was the last game of the season. Marty had already spoken with the coach, and they'd agreed that tonight would be his first and only game. He didn't have the stamina or speed to ever be able to actually contribute to the team, and Marty knew he was taking a spot that a more qualified player could have, so together they'd made the decision that tonight would be it.

The rest of the team filed out of the locker room and took their place on the bench, and the other starters joined Marty on the court. The guys wore their regulation jerseys, and Marty wore the one his teammates had given him while he was in the hospital. As they came out, each of the guys high-fived him and smiled as they took their places on the court. The sounds from inside the Brackett Field House were deafening and growing louder by the second. The starting players were announced over the PA system, and when they came to his name, the entire place erupted with applause and cheers. The campus newspaper had done an interview with him just the week before, so most of the other students knew his story.

What had surprised Marty most was the way the team took the news that he was gay. One or two of the guys had been standoffish at first, but it quickly became a nonissue when the other guys on the team not only acted as if it was no big deal, but were actually vocal in their opinion, in part thanks to Pat, who had actually blazed part of the trail for him.

The whistle blew and everyone got ready. The ref threw the opening toss, and Brackett came up with possession after the jump. All the players, including Marty, raced down the court. Ty had possession of the ball, and he passed it to Marty, who dribbled it and passed to Pat, who scored a sweet fifteen-foot jump shot. The coach immediately called a time-out. Marty then ran to the bench, and one of the other players came in. He'd started in his first, last, and only college basketball game. But he was on record with the NCAA and with the college as having been a starter. Marty sat on the bench and watched the game, rooting for his teammates at the top of his lungs through the entire first half of the game.

At the break, the team headed into the locker room for the coach's pep talk. "Stay here if you want," the coach told Marty as he passed. "It seems you have a rooting section who'd like to talk to you." Coach pointed to the far side of the court, where Marty saw a very familiar group of people. Marty walked over to where they were sitting in a huge group. His mother and father, Cassie, and Josh, all the guys from the ranch, and even Wilson in dark glasses, so no one would recognize him as Willie Meadows. Of course, Quinn was there as well and had already stood up and was making his way courtside.

"You did great!" Quinn told him, and before Marty could respond, the stuffing was being hugged out of him. Marty made his way off the court and up to where his biggest fans sat. Cassie hugged him hard, and even Josh seemed all smiles.

"How do you feel?" his mother asked, always worrying, as he approached,.

"I'm good, Mom," he said before hugging first her and then his father. Both his parents had come around. It had taken time, and for his father a great deal of explaining regarding his change of opinion, but his father simply explained it and then went on to win reelection. He'd told the family that this was going to be his last term in office, regardless.

"You looked good, son," his father said, beaming at him, and then at both of them as Quinn wound his arm around Marty's waist.

"Thanks, Dad. It was ceremonial, you know that," Marty said.

"There's nothing wrong with a little ceremony. Sometimes it tells you how much you're liked," his dad told him. "I know you have to get back soon, but after the game, I've arranged to take everyone to dinner. Your mother swears they aren't feeding you two enough and insisted we stuff you both full of food before we left." Sometimes it was good to have a father who was a senator, because once his father and mother began to understand what he and Quinn meant to one another, his father had stepped in and helped Quinn get a scholarship to Brackett's School of Veterinary Medicine. So when Marty had to leave the ranch to go back to school, Quinn had been able to go with him. Everything had indeed worked out, and it had all started the day he'd stopped hiding and started living.

Marty gave Quinn a quick hug and then bounded back down toward the court, turning to wave to everyone before joining his teammates on the bench. A short time later, the whistle blew and the second half began. The play went back and forth, but slowly and steadily Brackett pulled ahead—six points, eight points, twelve points. Play stopped as the other team called a time-out. Marty looked at the clock and saw there was just over a minute left to play. The Brackett coach pointed to Marty and told him to go in. Marty jumped off the bench and checked in at the scorer's table, enjoying the thrill of being on the court with the team once again.

After the requisite two minutes where they simply waited, the other team returned to the court, and play resumed. The ball was passed to him, and Marty took a single step, lifted the ball to take a shot at the basket, and then felt pressure on his back as he was pushed. His feet went out from under him and he tumbled lightly to the floor, the ball rolling away.

A whistle sounded and play stopped. Marty began to get up and saw the offered hand of the player who'd pushed him. Marty accepted it and was tugged to his feet.

"Take your two shots," he told Marty with a grin. Then he slapped Marty lightly on the back as he got into position. The referee handed him the ball, and Marty stood on the free throw line and looked up at the basket. The field house went nearly silent as Marty dribbled the ball a few times, concentrating on the basket. He lifted the ball and shot. As soon as the ball left his fingers, he knew it wasn't exactly right, but it was close. The ball sailed through the air and bounced on the rim of the basket, circling it before rolling away and off to the side.

"Aww" went up from the crowd, and the ref passed the ball back to him. Marty's heart pounded madly in his chest. He bounced the ball once and caught it. Something didn't feel right, and Marty looked to the side, locking gazes with Quinn across the field house. Everything was always all right when Quinn was there, and in those few seconds, he could feel Quinn like he was standing next to him. He cleared his mind of everything else, locked his eyes on the basket, and took his shot.

The ball sailed from his fingers in a perfect arc. It felt like one of those slow-motion moments in the movies, but Marty didn't need to see it. He already knew. The shot felt perfect.

Glancing to the side, he saw Quinn's mouth hang open and then saw him jump into the air. Turning back to the basket, he saw the ball swish perfectly through the basket, catching nothing but net. Marty jumped back as play resumed around him rather slowly. The game was largely over, and once the buzzer sounded, Marty once again looked into the stands. His friends and family were on their feet, yelling and cheering. Marty swore he could hear them calling his name over the rest of the crowd.

Marty took a few steps toward them before he was lifted off his feet and carried across the floor on the shoulders of his teammates. The game ball was thrust into his hands, and Marty grinned from ear to ear as he locked gazes with Quinn across the floor. For a second, out of the corner of his eye, he thought he saw Jefferson standing next to him, but when he looked again, he saw only Quinn beaming back at him.

ANDREW GREY grew up in western Michigan with a father who loved to tell stories and a mother who loved to read them. Since then he has lived throughout the country and traveled throughout the world. He has a master's degree from the University of Wisconsin-Milwaukee and works in information systems for a large corporation. Andrew's hobbies include collecting antiques, gardening, and leaving his dirty dishes anywhere but in the sink (particularly when writing). He considers himself blessed with an accepting family, fantastic friends, and the world's most supportive and loving partner. Andrew currently lives in beautiful historic Carlisle, Pennsylvania.

Visit Andrew's website at http://www.andrewgreybooks.com and blog at http://andrewgreybooks.livejournal.com/. E-mail him at andrewgrey@comcast.net.

The RANGE stories

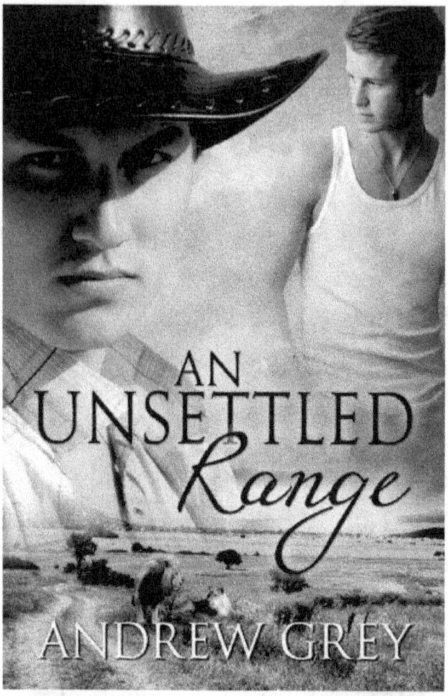

The ART stories

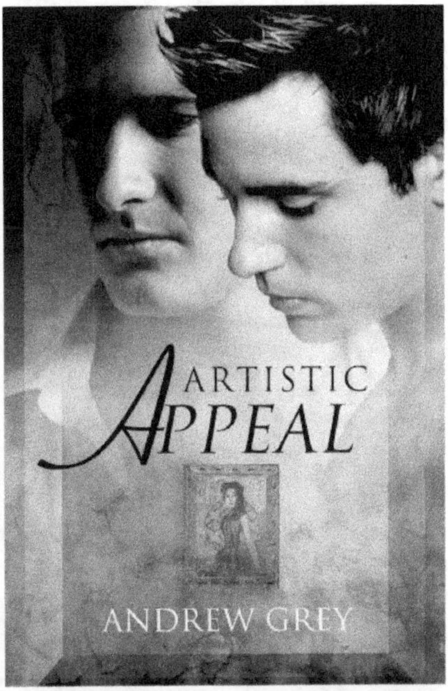

Now in Spanish, French, and Italian

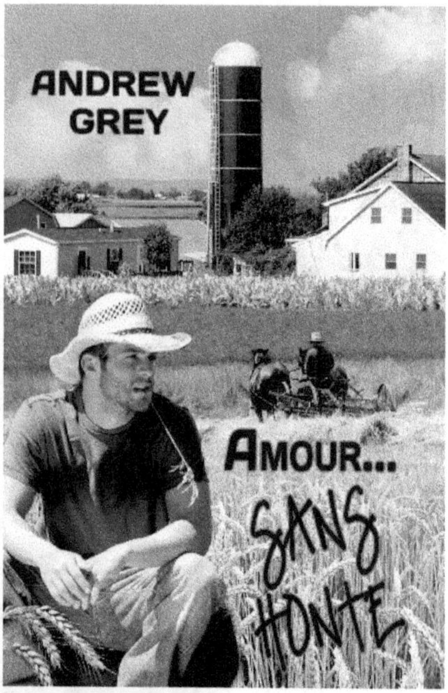

http://www.dreamspinnerpress.com

Also by ANDREW GREY

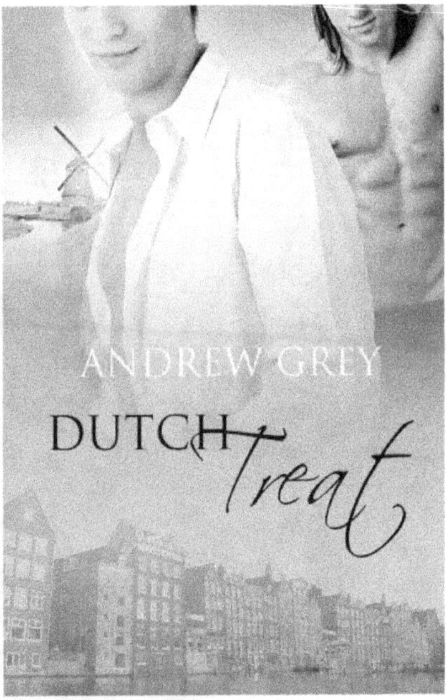

http://www.dreamspinnerpress.com

The LOVE MEANS… stories

http://www.dreamspinnerpress.com

Dreamspinner Press
For more of the
best M/M romance,
visit
Dreamspinner Press
www.dreamspinnerpress.com

www.ingramcontent.com/pod-product-compliance
Lightning Source LLC
Chambersburg PA
CBHW060057260626
47160CB00005B/1695
9781623800765